WITNESS PROTECTION

BROTHERHOOD PROTECTORS WORLD

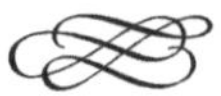

KANDI SILVER

This book is a work of fiction. Names, characters, places and incidents are products of the author's imagination or used fictitiously. Any resemblance to actual events, locales or persons living or dead is entirely coincidental.

BROTHERHOOD PROTECTORS

ORIGINAL SERIES BY ELLE JAMES

Brotherhood Protectors Series

Montana SEAL (#1)

Bride Protector SEAL (#2)

Montana D-Force (#3)

Cowboy D-Force (#4)

Montana Ranger (#5)

Montana Dog Soldier (#6)

Montana SEAL Daddy (#7)

Montana Ranger's Wedding Vow (#8)

Montana SEAL Undercover Daddy (#9)

Cape Cod SEAL Rescue (#10)

Montana SEAL Friendly Fire (#11)

Montana SEAL's Mail-Order Bride (#12)

SEAL Justice (#13)

Ranger Creed (#14)

Delta Force Rescue (#15)

Dog Days of Christmas (#16)

Montana Rescue (#17)

Montana Ranger Returns (#18)

Hot SEAL Salty Dog (SEALs in Paradise)

Hot SEAL Hawaiian Nights (SEALs in Paradise)

Hot SEAL Bachelor Party (SEALs in Paradise)

WITNESS PROTECTION

GIRLS WITH GUNS ~ BROTHERHOOD PROTECTORS CROSSOVER NOVEL

by Author

KANDI SILVER

PROLOGUE

RAIN POURED down over the streets of Bozeman, Montana, as CIA Officer Penelope "Lucky Penny" Moretti leaned against the metal of the partially open warehouse door. She steadied herself with the arm of the hand holding her gun. Penny lifted her free hand to her side and then pulled it away. Despite the weather, she glanced down at her palm and fingers, stained in crimson.

The bullet had hit her.

That explains the searing pain.

Fat thick rain splattered down and washed the blood away. At least she'd killed one before taking a bullet and killing the owner of the gun who'd planted one in what she hoped to god was only a flesh wound. The night sky and weatherly cloud cover made it impossible to discern if the blood was dark, indicating an organ.

She glanced up and down the dark alley. Other than the Montana rainstorm beating the ground in fat raindrops, she was temporarily alone. So far, she hadn't been followed by the Russian-speaking arms dealers.

However, it was only a matter of time.

What the hell went wrong? What were arms dealers doing at a drug bust?

Penny wasn't sure but knew hanging around debating would only put her in an early grave. She eased away from where she'd fallen back and reached into her cargo pants pocket. With a shaking hand, her finger wrapped one of the items. She withdrew the coin and dropped it, then took off at a run.

The soles of her unglamorous shoes hit the wet pavement, and the pain at her side reared its ugly head. Knowing she wasn't safe at her current location, she reaffirmed her grip around her gun and kept her run steady. There was something hypnotic about the downpour and her steady pace. She pressed her free hand against her side, hoping to stop the bleeding.

She needed something to focus on than her immediate danger and world warped around her. The only positive was her blood trail on the pavement would wash away her track. However, her pace slowed as her vision clouded and impaired. The wretched stench of nitroglycerine and sawdust assaulted her nasal cavity. Bright lights flashed on her face, blinding her temporarily.

I'm losing blood fast. Maybe too fast to get out of this cluster-fuck alive.

The car, which might be silver, stopped, and a man jumped out. "We've got to get you out of here," the voice barked in Russian.

Jesus!

There was something eerily familiar about the voice—belonging to her past. In the distance, there was more yelling. Broken English, mixed with something similar to Russian but not quite. She couldn't determine the language and had almost resigned defeat when the sound of semi-automatic rounds going off in the direction she'd come echoed through the rain. Despite the rain, the wind carried the wretched stench of nitroglycerine and sawdust; the scent of both assaulted her nasal cavity.

"We have no time, Penny," the voice in the dark stated with conviction.

How does he know my name?

Strong hands grabbed her, and opening doors echoed around her. Penny's body fell back, and the assault of the new car smell infiltrated her nasal passages. She put her head against something soft, which she could only conclude was the backseat, as more vehicle doors slammed and tires screeched on the wet asphalt after a jolt.

The vehicle was moving. Fast.

Street lights blurred with lightning in the sky through the rain-stained window. Hell, everything was becoming fuzzier.

"You're bleeding badly," the familiar voice stated. She couldn't fully recall. Rapid movement from the front seat startled her and something pressed against her side. "I need you to hold this."

Penny nodded as the man lifted her hand and put it on a towel against where she'd been hit by the bullet. It hurt like a son-of-a-bitch.

"We're being followed. Hold on!" A new voice spoke, only it was in a rush of Italian. Surely she was losing her mind because the voice reminded her of one of her mom's friends.

Italian? What the hell?

She knew that voice, though she hadn't heard it since childhood. "Zio?" Penny mumbled as her eyelids grew heavy.

From the corner of her memories, she could see the man standing on a flight of stairs but not make out his face. *"Nicholas, your Nonna was looking for you. Take Tally and Savvy and go wash your hands. We're going to be eating."*

"Penny, you need to hang in there," the initial voice barked at her. "I need you to stay awake."

She snapped her eyes open, fighting both nausea and fatigue. Her vision was blurred, and she couldn't focus, but she stared into the blue eyes. She didn't think she'd ever see him again. "Quinn?"

"Don't," the other man snapped in Italian and took a sudden wide turn, with more screech of tires.

Slowly it was impossible to keep her eyes open. Somehow, it was making her nausea worse. With her last ounce of strength, Penny stared at the man she never thought she'd see again. Her heart ached for Melanie. "Go home, Quinn. They need you."

Her lashes closed, and she needed to sleep.

"I think you've mistaken me for someone else," he answered in Russian.

"No." Penny tried to think, but it was impossible. "No, go home, Quinn," she mumbled as more memories flooded her, children laughed, and she missed cousins.

Penny always did at times like these.

CHAPTER 1

Lennox Peirce sat back in his leather desk chair inside his office and sipped his scotch. He glanced at the picture of his wife and wondered what she would think if she knew the mess he'd gotten the family into now.

True, things weren't always in our control.

It had been a long few months, and the situation was no better.

Over five hours ago, he'd gotten a joint call from the Director Danson of the FBI and Director George Lassiter of the CIA and briefed Lenny on CIA Officer Penelope "Lucky Penny" Moretti.

His sister's daughter and his niece.

Within thirty minutes, he had his team of four of his most elite on a private jet to Bozeman, Montana. They had landed and were at the crime scene, starting to piece what the hell had gone wrong and to find out what happened to Penny.

The phone on the desk's shrill ring echoed around the room he sat. His men and women under him always used his satellite phone or cellular phone. Few had the number on the desk. Only family and those in government who needed him.

He placed his scotch down and reached for the black handpiece. "Lennox," he greeted as he lifted the phone to his ear, then waited for what catastrophe had suddenly occurred since the last time his phone rang.

"Mio Fratello," a voice greeted, and Lenny's heart stopped.

Few men addressed him that way. Those from his boyhood days in New York, when he grew up in The Bronx. Lenny's family had been one of the few non-Italian families at that time in the neighborhood. The light accented tone was reminiscent of a voice he hadn't heard in over two decades. "Who is this?" Lenny asked in apprehension as he reached for his highball.

"I imagine you're starting to wonder if you're talking to a ghost, and you would be correct, Mio Fratello," the voice chuckled. "I wouldn't have risked this call. However, la famiglia prima di tutto."

"Family comes first," Lenny breathed as memories flooded into Lenny's mind.

"That is why we each made the decisions we have."

Memories flooded back, and Lenny downed the remainder of the scotch. He thought of the man who would be the one calling. "What's wrong?"

Other than more than I realized. Maybe I'm dreaming.

"Find a penny, pick it up, and all the day, you'll have good luck."

Lennox knew the rhyme all too well. It's how her niece got her code name. It stemmed from when she was a toddler. "She's alive?"

"For now, she has a bullet, from what I can tell, less than an inch below her spleen. It's not a straight-through. The bullet is inside her," the ghost at the other end of the line informed.

The news was bad. Very bad.

"Bring her in," Lennox demanded.

"Mio Fratello, I cannot," he answered. "My colleague and I have burned her clothes and cleaned her as best we could. She is in fresh attire. She'll be near Eagle Rock. There are amenities, but not enough to flag, like a city hospital, and I believe you have comrades in that vicinity."

Not many would suggest that or phrase it the way he had. Only an exclusive few.

"I can work with that," Lennox stated. "Why did you begin to irradiate?"

"Ask about the scientist," the ghost at the other end of the phone answered.

"Does this have something to do with Malebola? If so, you and your colleague will need a vaccine," Lennox warned.

Irony. Lenny was warning a dead man.

"My colleague, for the time, and I are already dead," he answered. "However, since I don't have time to argue with you, leave two in the glove compartment of your team's rental car. "Good bye Mio Fratello. I miss you."

I miss you too. Everyday.

So many emotions worked over Lenny. He pulled himself out of his chair, swiped his highball glass off the surface of his desk, then walked over to the decanter with the scotch. Lenny refilled his glass.

A real-life Ghost.

It wasn't possible. He'd been there the day of the massacre. He'd watched the man he loved as a brother bleed out as Lenny clutched the love of his life.

He took a swig of scotch, and his eyes watered. He knew it wasn't from the liquid turning to fire in his throat. So long ago, so many lives were destroyed by the assault and left children suffering in the aftermath.

How did he know about the Brotherhood? Or my team being in the area?

A ghost who had fluttered through the years in case reports. Every time an agent or officer on or off the books had been aided. The name Ghost always came up. However, nothing more was said, only that he appeared as quickly as he disappeared.

Tonight a voice beyond the grave had broken his silence because the officer in need was Penny.

He thought of the ramifications. Who would be his colleague, and how did the man or woman supposedly die?

The more he thought about things, the more questions were raised.

Javier Rodrigues was one of Lenny's team of four sent for processing the warehouse. The supervisory agent was a former Navy SEAL when he'd come into Lenny's life. A well-disciplined man, giving thanks and appreciation to the man Lenny now needed to call.

Ask about the scientist.

He slung back the remainder of the liquid in the glass, placed it down, walked over to his desk, and glanced at the cellular phone. Not this time.

He sat in his chair and reached again for the phone on his desk. He punched the number and waited for it to connect.

"What's on your mind, Lenny?" Chuck Johnson greeted from the other end of the line.

He didn't mean to sigh heavily, but hearing the other man's voice held some minor relief. "It's good to hear your voice."

"Let me step outside where I have better reception," he stated. "Kate, it's Lenny. I'll be back."

Lenny waited, and the sound of doors opening and closing echoed.

"Since you're calling me from your office phone, I know this isn't a social call," the man he'd known for over half his life stated.

"I'm afraid not, a situation has come up, and I need your help," Lenny informed.

"Is it personal or National Security?"

Lenny closed his eyes. "Both," he admitted. "My niece Penny was undercover, she was following drugs, and somehow Russian arms dealers got involved. There was a shootout in a warehouse in Bozeman, and Penny went MIA. Apparently intercepted by a ghost."

Chuck blew out a whistle. "You know we're getting too old for this, right?"

"Not that either of us would admit it to anyone but each other."

A deep chuckle erupted through the receiver. "That's a hell of a point." There was a stretched-out pause. "When you said the ghost, did you mean that metaphorically?"

"You're a former government agent. You've seen the folders and agent reports first hand," he stated.

Chuck cleared his throat. "You mean, *The Ghost*."

"He called me. He has Penelope and dropping her off near you, Chuck; he knew about you, the Brotherhood, or both," Lenny explained.

"So, who are you sending my way?" Chuck inquired.

"A Supervisory Special Agent Javier Rodrigues as soon as he is finished processing the warehouse, with his team."

There was a sneer at the end of the line. "Please answer me two questions," Chuck began. "First, is Rodrigues still as much of a smart-ass, and what does this have to do with national security?"

Lenny loosened his tie. "Sarcastic as ever; let me tell you a story about a bioweapon…."

CHAPTER 2

SUPERVISORY SPECIAL AGENT MACMILLION DEVEROUX pulled in front of the warehouse in Bozeman, Montana. The area crawled with local law enforcement and emergency crews. Javier Rodrigues was happy for once he wasn't in charge. The last time he had the lead, his team had been taken prisoner, and Javier had become friendly with a world-renown drug lord.

Javier, too, was a supervisory agent, only this time, the situation was different. "How do you want to do this, Mac?"

"The four of us are going in to process the scene, just like Lenny wants," he stated in his no-BS tone, then continued. "After that, we get all evidence back to the training compound before it starts raining again."

It finally has stopped coming down in buckets.

"Where the hell is Lennox's water cooler, boys?" Javier asked, thinking of his cousin Special Agent Jared Carter and his sidekick Special Agent Evan Darnell. "Why couldn't they gather the evidence instead of holding up a corner of the mansion back in sunny California?"

"Otherwise occupied," Foreign Operative Alexei Yuri bitched from the backseat. "Besides, they needed to protect Savannah, and Lennox wasn't up for her shooting someone she didn't like."

Javier snickered and glanced at Mac. "You're girl is one of a kind."

Mac nodded and grinned. "That she is."

"You're just pissy because Cowboy is on babysitting detail at a costly and exclusive elementary school until he's medically cleared," Special Agent Collin Lewis laughed from next to Yuri in the sedan's back seat. The vehicle blended locally but lacked comfort and leg room for men their size.

"He's got you there," Javier chuckled and glanced out the window. He stopped as his brain processed what he was witnessing. "What's hazmat doing here?" he asked aloud as he again became serious.

"No clue. Hazmat wasn't supposed to be part of the package," Mac groaned. "I hate surprises."

"Welcome to the club, brother," Javier agreed as Mac parked the vehicle and turned the engine off.

Yuri and Lewis opened the back doors and

unfolded their large frames. "I vote for an SUV. Next time Lenny comes up with one of his great field assignments," Yuri bitched.

"Amen to that," Lewis called while he stretched out his muscular frame. "I don't need to be processing crime scenes to remember why I became an agent. What kind of BS was Lenny feeding us this time? Doesn't he have probationary agents for this?"

"No clue, but I hate when he pulls stunts like this. I don't remember seeing a single hotel with a vacancy. There is no way in hell I'm sleeping in that thing," Yuri voiced, pointing at the rent-a-car. "Especially with the three of you."

Javier stared at the two men. "Are you ladies done bitching, or should I fetch one, if not both of you, a fashion magazine and a nail file?"

Mac threw his head back and laughed, then shut the driver-side door. "And here I thought you would get them some pretty panties."

He turned to his friend. "We haven't crossed the line for the scene. God knows I've got time to grab some, especially since we don't know if it's been cleared."

Lewis lifted his ball cap, ran his hand through his hair then replaced the hat on his head. "Are you two through busting Yuri's and my chops?"

"Depends if Hazmat and the locals will let us

have the scene," Mac told him with a sarcastic sneer.

Javier sighed and valued the men he was with. He'd worked with them along dangerous missions and deadly situations over the years. Javier stretched his back and thought of the last time the four were on assignment. Not long ago, in Columbia, at an auction gala for rich criminals.

He'd been one of the first to arrive when his team was taken. Javier had worked his way into the criminal's organization with his cover as another criminal.

Then everything changed.

Considering Javier and Mac's fiancée, Savannah had barely gotten out before the estate started to explode. The group of them was lucky to be standing there now. Despite processing a scene being Javier's least favorite thing to do, he was glad that the woman who'd saved his life over a year ago was under the protection of his cousin and Darnell.

Both would protect her at all costs.

"Might as well grab the gear and start flashing credentials," Yuri moaned as the group headed to the car's trunk. "I hate Cowboy for taking over my plushy job as a bodyguard and driver."

"Does Melanie or the housekeeper pack you a lunch too?" Javier teased as Mac popped the trunk with his remote. "You and Isadora can have gummy fruit snacks together."

"I forgot what smartass you are," Yuri told him as he removed a case holding chemical testing unit and another with miscellaneous gear.

They all removed the heavy metal cases. Mac had one and, with his free hand, slammed the lid down. They walked over to the scene tape and approached the officer in charge. "You must be the federal forensic team I was informed we'd have the pleasure of entertaining."

Entertaining?

The urge to punch the condescending man in uniform was overwhelming. By every ounce of restraint, Javier resisted. He'd promised Lennox and Mac no fist to cuffs, which meant no punching unsuspecting idiots.

No matter how much of an idiot the asshole might be.

"That'd be us," Mac told him while he reached into his pocket and withdrew his badge identification.

"Hazmat's cleared the scene, and my men have checked things out," the officer told him. "Of course, your director assured my captain you'd be sharing all findings."

Nope.

But the other man didn't need to know that. Javier glanced at the coroner's office sitting on the back of the bus. He blew out a breath and then glanced at the officer. "So what you're saying after hazmat cleared the area, they went and contaminated our crime scene?" Javier asked.

"We did our job," the officer stated with conviction.

"They contaminated our crime scene," Lewis stated and crossed the line heading toward the open warehouse door.

"Good job," Mac told the other man with a healthy dose of sarcasm, then he ducked under the yellow tape and followed Lewis.

Javier turned to Yuri. "I'll let you explain how we now need his and all of his men's shoe prints."

Yuri rolled his eyes as he turned to Javier. "No, I'm not—"

"Javier, I need my rectal thermometer. It's in one of the cases out there," Mac called.

The local officer winced and repositioned his stance, no doubt with his ass cheeks tensed together. That line worked every time.

Javier lifted his brows and couldn't control his sneer. Serves the man right for contaminating their scene. The locals had just created twice the work and tripled the evidence for Javier and the team.

He walked in and saw both men had started numbering evidence. Large cameras hung around both their necks. Javier's gaze surveyed the large warehouse, starting at the floor with the three dead bodies and working up and around the room. Turning his body, he explored the area behind him.

The good news was it was only one level, and the bad news was that the warehouse was empty except for the deceased.

Javier met Mac's gaze. "The locals would've walked through one of our only chances to get evidence, other than bullets in walls and blood splatter."

Mac merely nodded. "Lewis took photos in a path to the back. A small space, my guess storage, and a door leading to the alley."

"Do you think one of the local yahoos touched anything?" Javier set one of the cases down.

"I'll ask for copies of his men's fingerprints," Mac assured, shaking his head.

Yeah, that's what Javier thought too.

He carried the kit he'd packed down the winding path toward the area Mac had described. He placed the case down and pulled a pair of latex gloves out of his pocket. The cement by the back-door was discolored from a leaky seal at the bottom. With the amount of rain the area had experienced, he wasn't surprised he opened his kit and removed a light and a swab.

With eagle-eye precision, he started at one side of the area behind him, worked the light over the wall to his left, and slowly worked the flashlight to the door. Blood was on the metal where the door parted for entry and exit. Javier popped the swab and ran it across. Then sprayed luminal on the floor where the cement was discolored.

Sure enough. Splatters and drops revealed themselves in the water stain.

Nothing on the handle.

Javier stepped back and scanned the right side. More signs of the water, but in a different configuration.

The door had been open at one point for a while.

He glanced at the threshold and back to the water, leaving Javier wondering.

Was the owner of the blood coming, going, or watching?

CHAPTER 3

"CALL LENNY," Javier told Mac as Javier hurried over to where the other man removed a print off a gun magazine and closed the film. Mac held it against the device in his hand. "We've got a major problem," Javier told him with an edge of concern in his tone.

Mac's jaw set, looking up from the fingerprint recognition scanner in his hand. "What kind of problem?"

Javier lifted his gloved hand. Between his index and middle fingers was the item he'd picked up outside the alley door. The new copper penny glimmered under the lights.

"Officer Moretti was here," Mac stated with only minor relief.

Inhaling a deep breath, he nodded. "And is injured. She's bleeding, Mac, my guess pretty bad."

"Where was the penny in your fingers located?" his friend asked with apprehension.

"Out back in the alley," Javier replied as the device in Mac's hand beeped. "The rain washed most of the blood away. There's no trail and no dead or wounded body either."

Mac glanced down and stared at the scanner, then furrowed his brows.

"Is there a problem?"

A bleak expression worked across Mac's face, and he glanced back at Javier. "She was here with a dead man."

Yuri and Lewis approached, removing their masks and gloves as they joined Javier and Mac. "You need to call Savvy," Yuri informed. "We have a serious situation." He exchanged a hesitant look with Lewis.

"What could be worse than two dead Russian arms dealers, a dead Czech international drug dealer, Moretti was here, but no trace of her, dead or alive except a blood test confirming female blood type B-, and a shiny new copper coin? Plus, I just got a dead man's fingerprint, so again tell me, how much bigger than that?" Mac asked in concern.

Javier turned to Lewis as he sighed. "A chemistry set up and cocaine powder trace," Lewis began. "And another chemical compound in powdered form. He bagged his gloves and sealed the bag. "I'm sure hazmat removed a good chunk of evidence. There's a cot back there, which is even scarier. Someone slept in that room."

"Hazmat cleared this area," Mac reminded. "We're fine. Keep going."

"Only because they didn't realize what was here," Yuri told them solemnly, and Javier's neck hairs bristled.

The Navy SEAL still inside's instincts kicked in. Javier didn't need Yuri or Lewis to continue speaking. He already had some idea.

It was no coincidence Lenny had sent the four of them.

Lewis always had information on everything and everyone. Need to know? He was the man. Yuri was more than a bodyguard to a five-year-old but had Soviet and Eastern Bloc ties with backdoor channels. His family was a secret ally dating back to the cold war. Mac had both a scientific and medical background. Having spent time with Savannah as of late in the lab meant he was familiar with many of her creations.

"What?" The single word fell off Mac's tongue; however, his expression revealed dread.

Dread and suspicion.

"Let's just say it's a damn good thing we're all vaccinated," Lewis stated and lifted a test bag with purple liquid. "You better call your fiancée and tell

Savannah we suspect her biological weapon is now a powder."

Javier blew out a breath. "I don't know many chemicals that test that color. Only one. All men and women that contaminated the scene need vaccinations," Javier stated.

He'd seen the damage the weapon could do and now understood why Lennox sent him. He was familiar with Malebola, Savannah's accidentally created bio-weapon, but he was a former Navy SEAL. Undoubtedly, he'd be assigned to tracking CIA Officer Penelope "Lucky Penny" Moretti by the night's end.

She was the only one who would know what drugs and dead arms dealers had to do with Savannah's weapon.

Nothing good.

And everyone's day just got a hell of a lot worse. It's going to be a long night.

"I'll mask up and help Yuri and Lewis with the room. When you talk to Lenny, we'll need more vaccinations ASAP."

Mac nodded at Javier, then turned to Yuri. "Where are the officers you got shoe prints from?"

Yuri grinned, then lifted his brows. "Detained, all men, three of them complained, they needed to get back to, and I quote: the little woman back home."

Javier turned to Mac. "Can you imagine calling Savannah that?"

Mac turned and blinked. "Not unless I was asking to be shot."

Yuri and Lewis both agreed with Mac with nods and snickers. Then Yuri cleared his throat. "I have the officers fill out reports on what they saw and did when they arrived."

"Good way to keep them occupied," Lewis smiled. "I bet they feel like they are now part of a federal investigation."

"That was the plan," Yuri agreed.

"What do we know about Luck Penny?" Javier asked. "I never worked with her."

"Some say she is related to the Moretti crime family in New York," Lewis stated quietly. "She's a hell of an officer and a better operative."

The Moretti crime family? Interesting.

"Lewis and I worked with her in Russia about five, maybe five and a half years ago," Mac added.

However, it was what he didn't say that left Javier curious. "What else?"

"She, Quinn, and Matteo stayed in Moscow, and we joined you and Cowboy in Helsinki," Mac said. "She is that last person to see both Quinn and Matteo alive."

"Do you think this could be related to what transpired in that case?" Javier asked, trying to wrap his years of training and field experience around the mess they currently stood.

"I don't know, but I'll tell you something that goes no further than us. Lucky Penny is Lenny's niece and shares the same blood type as Savannah, B-, it's a Pierce family trait," Mac told them and inhaled deeply, then slowly exhaled.

A beep filled the room again from the scanner in Mac's hand. Javier held his breath as Mac glanced down; disbelief worked across his face.

"What?" Javier asked simultaneously as Lewis.

"Apparently, it was a dead man's party, or the scanner is malfunctioning," Mac sighed. "The fingerprint belongs to someone in the system. I can't access the information other than deceased."

"Don't you have Top Secret clearance from doing Savannah's security detail?" Yuri asked with a frown.

"We all do. I'm sure that's why the four of us are here. We all have the necessary clearance, unless," Javier replied, and his brain kicked into gear. "Is it compartmented?"

Mac only nodded. "Oh yeah, the only thing higher is level Yankee White."

For the second time in less than ten minutes, the hairs on the back of his neck raised. "That is working with The President and Vice President directly."

The guys all exchanged looks. None of them had that kind of clearance.

"Does Savannah?" Lewis asked.

"No. Savannah has a high level, but as far as I know not that high, or they would have given it to me. I went where she went, so it's a random guess," Mac responded. "Technically, I'm still on her detail."

"What the hell did we walk into?" Yuri demanded. "And why weren't we briefed accordingly."

Mac glanced at Yuri, then turned to Javier. "I don't think Lenny knows what the hell is going on."

Javier exhaled as his phone rang. He glanced at the number, and concern rolled over and down his back. "Rodrigues," he greeted into the phone and waited to find out why Chuck Johnson was calling.

Something inside him told Javier his night was to become a hell of a lot longer.

CHAPTER 4

DESPITE THE HAZE in Penny's brain and before she even opened her eyes, she knew she was no longer in the car or the room she'd been in. The smell was different. An abundance of pine infiltrated her nasal cavity. She'd been an officer and operative a long-time, and this was a new one even for her.

Sometimes a long-time resembled a lifetime.

She'd fine-tuned her senses. However, whoever made the relentless and continuous tapping sound, needed to stop—or risk death. All the sound was doing was making her head hurt more.

It sounds like a woodpecker.

The pain in Penny's side was excruciating, and the slightest movement reminded her she wasn't in any condition to fight or flight. That hadn't gone so well when she left the warehouse and had induced the craziest dreams.

More tapping and the sound of a bird chirping —singing, to be precise, like it was the feathered soul's last day on earth.

Penny struggled to open her eyes, but such a simple task was next to impossible and required much work. Despite her brain's fuzziness and sweat at her temples, she glanced around and noticed she was in a bedroom. Modest, but not a hotel—or a motel. She tried to move her arm on the side without the wound and discovered she wasn't cuffed or chained.

Where the hell was she?

Her tongue snaked out in an attempt to moisten her dry lips. She was incredibly parched and needed water. Penny struggled to sit up and epically failed. No strength whatsoever. Not to mention, it caused searing pain in her side. Her head fell against the pillow, and again her eyelids slammed shut. She digested what she had seen.

The room door had been open. Another indication Penny wasn't being held captive.

"We can't move her," a man's voice stated from another room, near and yet far at the same time.

She didn't recognize the voice.

"We've got to get the bullet out of her if she has any chance of surviving," the man spoke. His voice had a hint of an accent.

South American possibly?

His was the only voice. Was he on the phone? He had to be. Who was he talking to?

She didn't think she was in South or Central America. It didn't smell right—too heavy on the pine.

Forcing her lashes apart, she glanced to the window. The sun peaked through the slit of the heavy curtains in the room. It was daylight. She'd survived the night, but where the hell was she?

Who owned the voice? More so, where the hell was her gun?

With every ounce of strength, she maneuvered her body upright on the bed. Her body screamed in pain, reminding her she had been shot. The lightheadedness she experienced forced Penny to face the reality that she'd lost a lot of blood.

The odds currently weren't in her favor. Out of all the ways she figured she'd die, this current scenario wasn't one of them. She brushed the wet hair off her face and realized the skin was hot to the touch.

I have a fever.

Penny knew she was probably getting an infection from her injury—or worse, the bullet was still inside her, and her body was fighting to reject it. Not good either way. Her legs weren't bound either, but she doubted she had the strength to stand.

Hell, she was battling to stay conscious.

Heavy boots scuffed against the wooden floor, and she guessed the boots' owner was heading toward her. Fear and her instinct to fight motivated her to move her legs enough to get one foot on the floor.

A large frame filled the threshold of the room. "Penny," the man called. "What are you thinking?" he gasped, then hurried over to where she was on the bed.

She wanted to fall back from exhaustion but stared at the man. Obviously, she still had a pulse because the man was gorgeous. Why did bad guys always have to be good-looking?

Wait, did he use my name?

"You need to rest," the huge man stated. He had to be at least six-foot-two. "I'm not going to hurt you, Penny."

He did it again. The man said her name. She tried to speak, but her throat and mouth were too dry. "Water," she choked out.

A sad expression worked across his handsome face. "You shouldn't don't move. I'll get something," he assured, then left the room.

Part of her wanted to cry, the other fight. She tried to move her left leg and get her left foot on the ground. Sweat formed at her temples, and the injury to her side reared its ugly head. Instinctively her hand went to her side. Beneath her palm was a padding of gauze and tape.

The man returned to the room, and displeasure worked across his face. "I told you not to move." He placed a water glass and a pink sponge stick on the nightstand near the lamp. She could use the lamp as a weapon. Only with how slow her reflexes were —screw it.

Penny reached for the lamp, curled her fingers around it, and started lifting it.

"Not today, Officer," the man stated, and his strong hand removed the lamp from her hand. He placed it back down, then turned and put a hand on his denim-covered hip. "Penelope Moretti, my name is Javier Rodrigues. I work with your uncle Lennox Pierce and have worked with your cousin Savannah."

She shook her head. "Lie," Penny croaked and attempted to move her leg again, but she didn't have the strength.

"I thought Mac was kidding when he said that stubbornness was a Pierce trait," Javier replied as he reached for the water and stick. He dipped the sponge tip in the water and lifted it to her lips. "Please."

How can I trust him? He lied. How does he know Mac?

However, without water, she wouldn't be able to speak. Penny opened her mouth and allowed Javier to dampen her lip. She sucked some of the liquid from the sponge. It absorbed into her tongue almost immediately, and Penny eased her head back. She realized that both hands were braced on the bed, maintaining her balance.

Javier dipped the sponge into the water and lifted it to her mouth for a second time.

Penny again took the little water he offered. She struggled and swallowed. "You lied," she whispered.

"I promise you I haven't. I respect your Uncle Lennox too much," Javier stated and repeated the process by dipping the stick in the water. His expression revealed nothing.

This time after she swallowed, she knew her words would be limited. "Savannah, not an agent," she rasped and looked at the glass of water in his hand.

"I didn't lie," Javier told her. "She went to free US agents stuck on Serpentine's compound. I was one of the agents, as was Mac. She rescued us." A look of debate worked across his face. "I know you want to fight Penny. I know you don't know who to trust as much as you want me to pass this glass of water. I need you to trust me because you still have that bullet in you, and it needs to come out."

Fear coursed through her. "No hospital."

He shook his head. "No, too risky, and I can't remove it because it's too close to your spleen."

"No trust," she muttered, and her head became fuzzy. Sweat dripped from her temple and ran down the side of her face.

Javier set the glass and sponge stick down. "You're fighting a fever and in excruciating pain." He rose from where he was crouched in front of her. "I'll be right back," he told her and hurried out of the room.

Penelope glanced at the glass of water and knew she would have to steady herself with her left arm if she reached for it. She needed to get out of here. He was lying.

Savannah was a scientist, not an agent.

The man who called himself Javier wasn't even a good liar. Out of all of her cousins she had, some actual agents, he chose the antisocial science geek.

True, trying to escape would be her death. She wouldn't get far. In some ways, it would be a relief. She always figured she'd be alone when she died. Not how she wanted to die, just how it would be.

How many times had she nearly missed death's door?

More than a cat has lives.

Javier's boots scuffed against the wooden floor. Again he approached with everything inside her; Penny reached for the water glass and lifted it. She brought the mirror up to her mouth and gulped back the liquid. The man stepped to the threshold, and she hurled the glass at him.

He dodged and started to laugh. "Wow, never has the family resemblance been more prevalent. You're in worse shape than I thought because your cousin threw a beaker full of powder at me and didn't miss."

Nausea kicked Penny in the gut. Gulping the water had been a bad idea.

"You gulped back some of the water," he stated and stepped closer.

Penny was back to staying seated by the strength of her arms. She wasn't sure how much more she could take. "What powder?"

"A special Savannah blend of itching powder that affected the skin similar to poison ivy and was derived from the plant I discovered shortly after."

Now that sounds like Savvy.

"She didn't take protection detail gracefully," he informed and stepped over to where she sat. Again he crouched down and lifted a cold cloth to her head. "Now, I'd lay down my life for her more than ever."

The tattoo on the inner side of his arm on his bicep stopped her heart. Nausea sucker punched her, and she titled forward, bringing up the water she had gulped down and depositing it near Javier's boots. Her whole body felt like it was on fire, and her strength was fading. She closed her eyes. "I'm dying," she choked out.

"Not if I can help it," Javier told her. "Let's get you comfortable and stop using your strength. Let me do the heavy lifting."

She again met his dark brown gaze. "Marine?"

"Former Navy SEAL, just like your uncle," he told her, placing the cloth on the table.

Very few know that.

"Semper Fi," she whispered and struggled to lift a hand to his tattoo.

"Semper Fi," Javier repeated.

Fatigue hit Penny like a brick to the head, and she started to fall forward. Javier's strong arms captured her, and she rested his head against his shoulder. "I don't want to die alone."

"You won't be," Javier told her, wrapping his arms around her protectively. "I made your uncle a promise; you won't die on my watch."

For a fleeting moment, Penny almost believed him.

CHAPTER 5

JAVIER SAT in the chair playing a game on his phone in the guest room of his cabin. A small three-bedroom two bath retreat. He never thought that the place he'd bought just to go fishing and get away from working for the government would be a sanctuary to a CIA foreign operative.

Someone other than him.

On the bed, Penny tossed slightly. "Go home, Quinn," she mumbled. "They need you."

His heart stopped beating. Suddenly the match-three game on his phone didn't exist. He stared at the injured woman on the bed.

God, she's beautiful.

Her features resembled Savannah to some extent, like the big brown eyes and the nose. The rest, down to her dark auburn hair sprawled across the pale peach-colored pillow case, made her unique.

"Zio, non lasciarmi morire,"she whispered.

His knowledge of Italian wasn't inadequate, but he could speak it and understand what was being said after years of working in Europe. The language was a romantic language like the Spanish he'd learned growing up on the Army base in Puerto Rico.

Uncle, don't let me die.

Unusual dialogue, even for a dream. Maybe he shouldn't have said what he did about Lenny. However, she'd seen Javier's tattoo. But why was she calling Lenny zio? Respect or more? Never in the years had Javier known Savannah, had she spoken Italian to her father. Maybe it was the pain killers Mac had left with him.

Either way, interesting.

"I thought you were dead," she murmured in Russian.

Again, Javier's heart stopped as he thought of Quinn. A pathetic whimper escaped Penny's full lips, and she started to cry. The soft sob sound affected Javier to the root of his soul. Immediately, he was out of the chair and to the side of the double bed. "Shh," he comforted and brushed the hair off her face. She was burning with fever, and the antibiotics were becoming less effective.

Mac had warned him.

Javier hurried to the hall, grabbed another towel, and soaked it in cold water. He wrung the majority out, then again was by Penny's side. He placed the cloth on her forehead and prayed she didn't go into shock. He closed his eyes and recited words to a prayer he learned as a child in Puerto Rico.

"You're scaring me," she whispered, lifting her hand and covering his interlocked fingers.

He opened his eyes and met her doe-like gaze. "I could say the same about you," he whispered in Italian.

"How are you still conscious?"

"The room is a bad roller coaster, but chalk it up to fire in my Italian blood and Pierce stubbornness," she confessed. "Call my brother. He can remove the bullet."

He remembered the conversation with his friends in the warehouse. "Who is your brother?" he asked, trying to keep his hesitation out of his tone.

"Rafael Moretti, a doctor at St. Teresa of Avila hospital in New York, Upper Manhattan," she sighed in a barely audible tone.

"The patron saint of headaches," Javier whispered.

"You haven't met my brother. Rafe *is* a headache," she admitted before her lashes fluttered closed, and she again fell to sleep.

For the first time since he had been young and dumb, a smart-mouth punk at boot camp, he felt like he was over his head. He'd seen some life-or-death situations and lost colleagues in front of his eyes, but this was new, different, and he wasn't sure how. Javier waited for Penny's breathing to fall into a steady rhythm.

He closed his eyes and decided to make a call. Rising from where he'd knelt beside her bed, Javier crossed to where he'd left his phone on the rocking chair and scooped it up. He closed the game he'd been playing and punched Mac's number.

"Deveroux," his friend greeted. "What's going on, Rodrigues?"

Javier sighed. "She needs the bullet removed," he began.

"I know. I'm working on that now," Mac replied. "I'll be coming back to Montana."

Javier debated his following words and glanced at the beauty sleeping. Her color was pale. "She wants her brother Rafael Moretti. He's a doctor at St. Teresa of Avila."

"A hospital in New York, yep, I know," Mac finished.

The dude's been spending too much time with Lewis. He's becoming Mr. Know-It-All.

Mac sighed, which was never a good sign when it resembled defeat. "In your conversation, as she asked for her brother, did she by chance mention their father is Lorenzo Moretti, consigliere to Don Salvatore "Sam" Giordano, a notorious mafia godfather?"

Javier pursed his lips. "Never came up because she passed out again."

"Convenient," Mac scoffed.

What the hell was Mac's problem, and why was he acting so strange? "How did you find this out? Did Lenny talk?"

"Not exactly, Savannah did," Mac replied. "Lenny doesn't know I'm here."

Oh, not good.

Javier knew the agent he was on the phone with and the pretty scientist well and regretted his next question. "Where are you?"

"Upper Manhattan," he mumbled. A door opened and closed on Mac's end.

"You're at the hospital?" he asked in surprise. "The one Rafael Moretti works at?"

"Yes, against my better judgment," Mac admitted, then groaned. "And he has spotted me walking down the hallway toward him."

Javier detected the edge in Mac's tone.

"Rafael Moretti," his buddy greeted, still holding the phone.

"You must be the chooch who dared to ask my cousin Savannah to marry him before she even introduced you to her family," the man Javier guessed was Rafael told Mac.

That's it, Mac; piss off the mob; we don't have enough problems.

"Savannah said you'd be coming," Rafael informed. "Who the hell is on the phone? That you couldn't hang up with, and again you demonstrate bad manners since I highly doubt it's my cousin."

This guy is not happy. Not good. Thank heavens Mac is an elite agent.

"It's not Savannah. A friend is trying to keep your sister alive and protect her simultaneously. So, cut the overprotective BS until we're on a flight out of here."

Mac, Mac, Mac, that is not how to win friends and influence people. Not that he should make friends with the mob—he is marrying into it. How did Lennox get his job?

"Allow me to remind you, he is the mob, and you didn't meet the family before you proposed. What the hell were you thinking?" Javier demanded.

He needed a vacation. Wait, that's what this cabin was for.

Dammit!

"I love her," Mac stated quietly.

Silence.

Javier knew his friend meant the words, but why was Savannah circumventing Lennox?

"I'll take that phone now," Rafael informed Mac.

Before Mac could reply, the phone transferred hands. "Hello, who am I speaking with?"

Polite, with an assertive tone. Here goes nothing.

"Javier Rodrigues, former Navy SEAL, and government agent, your sister got tangled up in a gunfight, she was shot, and if calculations are correct, the bullet is still inside her." Javier swallowed before continuing. "It's close to her spleen." He glanced at Penny and closed his eyes. "Your sister asked for you."

"Keep her alive until I get there," Rafael ordered in a cool crispness, which left no room for debate. "I'll be there as soon as possible, and Agent Rodrigues, as I said, keep her alive, or our meeting will be unfortunate."

Did he just threaten me?

Javier didn't know. What he did know was that the call had ended.

"Zio, non lasciarmi morire," Penny rasped and her breathing became uneven. "Perché ci hai lasciato," she sobbed and started to cry.

Again she murmured in Italian, *Uncle, don't let me die,* followed by *why did you leave us?*

He inhaled a deep breath, and his mind started sorting out what he knew and didn't. Javier's gaze rested again on the dying CIA operative. He grabbed the cold cloth and again dabbed Penny's head.

Penny's eyes startled open. "Javier, don't leave

me," she begged and rested her hand on his holding the cool cloth.

"I'm not going anywhere," he assured the beauty before again her eyes fluttered closed.

Savannah, what did you get me into?

CHAPTER 6

THE CABIN DOOR opened behind Javier, who sat on the steps. By footsteps alone, he knew they belonged to Savannah. "Mac and Rafe are closing up, Penny. She's stable, and they got the bullet, and it wasn't as deep as they thought it might be."

Only minor relief worked over Javier as the pretty blonde scientist sat on the steps next to him. "And Rafael hasn't stabbed Mac yet with a scalpel?"

"That's not Rafe's style," Savannah sighed. "He'd slit his throat from ear to ear then make it look like natural causes by some miracle."

Her words were of little comfort to Javier. So many questions ran through his mind. "How did your dad get the job he has with mafia ties?" He glanced at the woman beside him. Eyes and nose like the beauty in life-saving surgery.

"My dad's sister, my aunt Charmaine, married

Lorenzo Moretti, one of the guys he grew up with in The Bronx," she whispered. "As far as my dad, he, like you, is a former Navy SEAL. He's the best and trains men like you to be better than him." The last part came out with minor hostility. Savannah pulled her frame off the steps and started to pace.

"Why did you circumvent your dad?" Javier inquired. The question that had been on his mind since talking to Mac.

"When my dad sent you, Lewis, and Cowboy with Yuri to do forensics, my gut sucker-punched me. The last time I had that feeling was when Mac went to Serpentine's compound," she admitted softly.

Not good. What the hell?

"I heard my father tell Mac to leave two vaccine vials for Malebola in the glove compartment of the rental. All four of you had been vaccinated, so I was confused. Who would they be for? You and the team were sent with enough for anyone who might have come in contact should evidence of my weapon show up at the scene. Keep in mind, there are still unaccounted vials, which went to people other than Serpentine."

Javier noticed the duress on her face. "Go on, Savvy."

"The guys came back from Bozeman, shaken. I've only seen that much fear in Mac's eyes once before. The night turncoat Agent

Bronson Jefferson tried to take me from an event," she admitted. "Yuri was bothered by something. He does that speedy brow frown and plays it cool, then repeats the gesture several times, but there was something in his eyes. Mac told me about the Yankee White clearance on the print he ran. My father doesn't even have that level."

Heavy steps echoed inside the house, but it didn't seem like a struggle. So Javier didn't jump to Mac's rescue.

"Do you trust your father?" Javier wondered aloud.

"Normally, I'd say yes, but I don't think he knows what's happening. Which is scary, the man usually knows, before government agencies, when it comes to domestic issues." Savannah kicked a rock lightly with the toe of her hiking boot. "There is talk my aunt married into the mob, but…." Hesitation worked over her face and didn't add whatever she'd been thinking.

Javier glanced at Mac and Rafael by the screen door inside the cabin.

"So I have no answer to your question on how my dad got his job," Savannah continued. "But if I've learned one thing over the last year and a half, the supposed good guys can be the worst of people, and even bad guys can have a heart and do good things."

The two men in the house exited quietly and even shut the door without a sound.

"Sure, my Zio Lorenzo might be Italian mafia, which would make him a bad guy, yet his son saves lives for a living, and his daughter is one of the top CIA operatives. My father is Lennox Pierce, and I work for the government, and yet I created one of the most deadly bioweapons on the planet by accident—mind you. Still, it has already killed people. So what does that make me?"

"Instincts like none other," Mac replied from behind Javier. "Logan was right about that."

Javier stood and turned toward the two men. "How's Penny?" he didn't mean to reveal so much concern in his tone. However, there was something special about her, and he wanted to know what that was.

"Stable. I'm hoping Penny stays that way. I'm surprised her infection wasn't much worse. Mac says he left you with some antibiotics, thank you for administrating them. I'll stay the night, monitor her, then leave in the dark tomorrow night, as long as she shows progress," Rafael informed less crisply than before. He stared at Javier with penetrating scrutiny. "My sister said your name before we gave her anesthetic."

"She's worked with many of my friends," Javier began maintaining eye contact with Dr. Moretti. Mob or not, Javier wouldn't let the man intimidate him. "She's good at what she does. I didn't know until last night she was Lennox's niece."

Rafael narrowed his gaze. "Fair enough." He then turned to Mac. "You mentioned Logan. His last name wouldn't happen to be Angelo, would it?"

Mac blinked at the other man. "Normally, I wouldn't answer that question, bad memory and all, but I also know his dad and your Zio Lenny grew up in the same neighborhood. Yeah, he's a good friend and one hell of an agent. I also know he would do anything for Penelope and Savannah both."

"Carlo Angelo, I also call *Zio*." Rafael clarified. "Zio Carlo, his wife, and Logan are *la Famiglia*, as far as my family is concerned," Rafael stated with a firm tone. He then turned to Javier. "Tell me, SEAL, do you feel the situation is off as much as Savannah?"

Logic told him telling a mobster national secrets was a real dumbass idea, however…. "Yeah, I do. Your sister is CIA, and she had no business working on American soil, so my big question is, why was she? Something had her follow a trail back stateside."

"Or someone," Savannah stated quietly.

What does she know that the rest of us don't?

Javier looked at the rented moving truck and how it had pulled up with the medical equipment and Penny's brother. "How did you mobilize so fast and without Lenny knowing?"

"Let's just say Savannah circumvented more than her dad," Mac supplied and exchanged a look with Savannah. "She called Rafael and sent me on a jet to get him, knowing he might need another set of hands with medical knowledge. She then met us in Bozeman."

Rafael stepped down the steps and walked over to where Savannah stood as Mac closed the distance and relocated himself next to Javier. There was something in his eyes that Javier couldn't identify, but if instincts were right, there was more to Dr. Moretti than met the eye.

"What's bugging you?" Rafael asked Savannah quietly.

She shook her head. "I'm not sure. There's more to this. I feel it. Dad has been super quiet since he sent the team to the warehouse, I have so much evidence to process, and I'll be busy doing that for the next year because the federal agencies are still processing stuff from Serpentine's compound."

Javier exchanged another look with Mac.

"You know, I need to notify Padrino of what has transpired. He isn't going to be happy," Rafael sighed and studied Savannah. "Do you think this is personal?"

"Padrino doesn't need to know," she protested.

Rafael shook his head. "No, I'm telling him

because if I don't, and he finds out, then finds out I knew, it will not end well. Nonna has a magic wand with your name on it for not bringing your boyfriend home to her."

Javier frowned and exchanged a look of curiosity with Mac, who wore a confused expression, then both rested their attention back on the cousins. "Magic wand?" he braved to ask.

"A hand-carved wooden spoon, which she no doubt wants to crack across my ass," Savannah harrumphed.

"Ah, my Abuela has one of those, she refers to as the palo sabio—meaning *wise stick,*" Javier informed. "Nice to see some things are universal."

"Indeed," Rafael grinned.

Savannah rolled her eyes, and a thoughtful expression crossed her pretty face as she focused her attention on her cousin. "In answer to your question, my knee-jerk reaction would be no," she stated quietly.

There was a brief moment of silence as they waited for her to continue.

"But?" Javier, Mac, and Rafael asked simultaneously.

Savannah darted her gaze over the three men. "That was bordering on surreal and frightening you all know me that well. I've had the thought cross my mind; maybe it is personal, but how?"

Silence again, this time, because no one had answers.

Rafael turned to Javier. "Answer me something. Do you concur with Mac and our mutual friend Logan's opinion of Savannah's instincts?"

"I do. Savannah fired the kill shot on Serpentine, his forehead dead center," Javier stated, again meeting the mob doctor's gaze.

"Ciccio, you are lovely and deadly, never has the family resemblance to my sister been so uncanny," Rafael smiled. "The others will love this information. You make our family proud." The smile fell from his face, and anger etched in his features. "Of course, hell will be paid in questions about what your ass was doing on Serpentine's compound."

"Extraction and detonation," she answered without missing a beat.

Rafael shook his head. "How do you suggest I tell Padrino of such things?"

Savannah flashed her cousin a smile. "You could always try keeping your mouth shut."

Rafael didn't respond as the two stared each other down.

Wait, Padrino means godfather, not grandfather. Got to love the mob.

Fatigue worked over Javier, but it wasn't the first time he was tired and had a job to do—especially when he was active as a SEAL. There were also the countless times since he'd become an agent. It was then his brain digested what Rafael had said. "Did you call her Ciccio?"

"It is an endearment in Italian," Dr. Moretti explained. "Savannah is the youngest and was always sweet and thoughtful. It translates to *Sugar*."

Mac grinned. "That explains a lot."

Rafael glared at Javier's buddy. "How so?"

"It's what Mac calls me," Savannah stated quietly. "He has since the moment he met me."

Rafael nodded his head. "Mac, you're proving not to be a chooch after all. I'll say a good word for you with *la Famiglia*."

Slightly reassuring for Mac.

"I assure you," Javier began. "Mac has a lot of common sense, even though I question him for not introducing himself to your family sooner."

My guess is he didn't know who the next of kin was.

"Nor did he ask for permission to marry her. You, however, are showing signs of exhaustion," Rafael observed. "Get some rest, SEAL, while you have back up."

Was that an order? Yeah, it was.

Mac nodded. "He's right. I've got your six," he assured.

Javier turned to Savannah. "Do you need a gun?"

"No, I've got my .38 and my Walther PDP Compact," she assured. "Plus, I already found the cutlery drawer. I'm good."

A mortified expression worked over Rafael's face, and his mouth dropped open, followed by a rant in Italian that involved Nonna, Mary and all saints, and the love of God. Not necessarily in that order.

Javier controlled the urge to laugh while Mac snickered.

Rafael cast Savannah a displeased expression. "Don't tell me Logan taught you his fork trick?"

Savannah smiled at her cousin. "Okay, I won't," she grinned, then walked toward the cabin.

"You're not like them," Rafael tossed his head in Mac and Javier's direction. "You're not like Penny or the others. You're not an agent."

Hold up, others? Interesting.

Mac picked up on it and shot a questioning look in Javier's direction.

Oh yeah, there was a lot they didn't know.

Stopping in her tracks, Savannah shifted and blinked at Rafael. "Thanks for the reminder," she told him with a solemn expression and venom coating her words. "I'm going to check on Penny," she said to the men and opened the door.

Apparently, her cousin hit a nerve. More like jumped on it.

None of the men spoke. No doubt, both Mac and Rafael had picked up the bitterness in her tone. Instead, they waited until Savannah had gone inside, and her gentle scuffs echoed down the hallway. Rafael stepped over to where Javier and Mac stood on the porch steps. "What does she know that we don't?"

Mac shook his head. "I wish I could tell you, but I'm wondering the same thing." His gaze drifted to the door Savannah had entered through.

Javier nodded. "I think it's the big question. One that I know will open a whole can of worms."

By the expressions on the other two men's faces, they too agreed.

"We need to find out," Rafael stated as Mac nodded in agreement.

Javier concurred. "That we do. Sooner rather than later. I feel this is just a piece of the bigger picture."

"Same," Rafael admitted. "And I don't like walking into something without all the information."

"Welcome to the club," Javier replied.

Whatever was going on wasn't good. God help them all.

CHAPTER 7

Penny inhaled a deep breath. The room smelled sterile. However, the essence of pine still remained. Her ears picked up a steady electronic beep she couldn't place and didn't remember hearing before. She opened her eyes and was still in the room she was in earlier. Her torso had been slightly elevated with pillows.

Despite feeling groggy, the fuzzy-headedness had alleviated to some extent. Penny turned her head, and her gaze rested on her cousin Savannah who unfolded herself from the rocker and smiled. "You're awake," she stated the obvious softly.

Not since she was a child had she been so happy to see her younger cousin. She was alive and safe. "Savvy, Javier didn't have to call you," she exclaimed, feeling slightly emotional as Savannah came and sat on the edge of the bed.

Her cousin curled her fingers around Penny's hand that had intravenous taped to her wrist and her finger with a clamp, obviously connected to the vital statistics monitor. "He didn't. He called Mac."

Her heart skipped a beat. "I trust Mac."

"And he and I both trust Javier," Savvy insisted. "He's a former Navy SEAL."

Penny nodded slowly. "I saw his tattoo. It's similar to the one your dad has on his triceps, Semper Fi. He isn't hard on the eyes unless my vision was awful."

Savannah giggled. "Your eyesight was really off because Javier's looks lean more to the gorgeous side of the hotness scale."

Yeah, that's what I thought.

Unfamiliarity worked over her, and varying emotions worked over her. "Am I dying?"

"Thankfully, you're going to live," her brother called from the room's threshold.

Rafael's large frame stepped into the room, and a broad smile illuminated his blue eyes. "How are you feeling?"

"Better now," she replied, feeling a small joy to see her brother. He'd always done his best growing up to protect her. Though he wasn't happy when she told him she'd been invited by the CIA to join them.

Too much risk.

Not just for Penny but the family. A family with

a lot of secrets. Sometimes too many. She darted a glance to Savannah. There was so much she didn't know—and with the grace of God, never would. Zio Lenny and the family had made sure.

Mac and Javier entered the bedroom. They were close to her brother's height, if not a bit taller, and had broad shoulders in similar stature as Rafe. The room suddenly shrunk, with the three large men taking up space. "Good to see you're still the Lucky Penny," Mac chuckled.

"I was in capable hands," she assured and met Javier's dark gaze.

Oh yeah, Savannah was right. He was gorgeous and looked just like the guy in her dreams. Even through his fitted t-shirt, she could determine how defined his abdominal muscles were. Her heart skipped a beat, and the monitor double beeped.

"I'm sorry I threw the glass at your head," she apologized.

Javier chuckled, and he smiled, making him even better looking. "Thankfully, you missed."

"And wasn't...what did you say, poison ivy powder?" she asked, trying to recall what he had told her.

"Who the hell threw poison ivy powder at you?" Rafe asked Javier with a furrowed brow.

"Your cousin, when I was assigned to her security detail," Javier clarified.

Rafael turned a scornful glare on Savannah.

"That nonsense stops! If you're assigned security detail, you take it with grace." He wasn't happy and turned to Javier. "Did it have the same effect as skin exposure to the plant?"

"Oh, yeah," he answered, thinning his firm lips. "Just a bit more concentrated."

Rafe was pissed. He pursed his lips, shook his head, and cast Savvy his death glare. "Wait till I tell Padrino that one."

"It was over a year and a half ago, Cowboy wasn't around, and the threat was minor," Savannah stated with blatant hostility.

"Was it minor?" Rafe asked, turning his steadfast glare on Javier.

The former Navy SEAL sighed. "No." He darted a glance to Savannah, then met Rafe's sapphire gaze. "Her biological weapon Malebola was stolen from the CDC's high-containment lab in Atlanta. We knew some of it ended up in Serpentine's hands. However, since we've learned there is more out there. People wanted her alive, including Serpentine at that time. We feared a kidnapping attempt."

"I understand that information is classified. Thank you for your honesty," Penny's brother told Javier. "I know it was a tough call, but it proves you understand, la famiglia prima di tutto."

"Family comes first," Javier repeated in English.

Rafael turned to Savannah. "That is not what I

consider minor." He then cast Penny his scrutinizing stare. "Did you know?" Anger coated every word.

Dammit to all screaming hell. Happy to see him, but he can leave now.

Penny sighed and suddenly experienced fatigue again. She also knew her brother would act like a dog with his favorite chew toy and not let the question go. "I'd heard rumors, but eventually, I found out it was true. She was safe, under protection by men Zio Lenny trained and trusted." She turned to Javier. "My guess the first time by you."

The sexy man met her gaze and smiled. "You guessed right."

She forced herself to ignore the flutters in her stomach, but the heart monitor double beeped. Penny decided the machine would meet its demise. How dare it rat her out. Especially when both Rafael and Mac turned to the device.

One a doctor, the other almost one.

"I feel like la Famiglia should send out apology baskets in advance to those who are supposed to be protecting you," Rafe exclaimed at Savannah. He was beyond unhappy and continued to demonstrate his pissed-off demeanor. "Who is your current security detail, and where the hell are they?"

"Technically, that would be me," Mac confessed.

Rafe focused a deadly stare on Mac. "No

wonder you didn't answer me with anything further than through her father when I asked how you two met. Tell me, did you guard her from over the top in bed?" Her brother continued to rant.

"Of course not!" Savvy snapped in a temper, coming to a standing position and pulling herself up to full height in an attempt to square off with Rafe, who, like the other men, towered over Savannah.

Here we go again!

Savannah met Rafe's gaze and flashed him a bitchy smile. "First, I invited him into my bed; for the record, sometimes I'm on top."

Mac cringed, and Javier buried his face in his hand. Suddenly Penny was glad Nicky and Vince weren't there. Things would be so much worse. However, she gave her cousin credit; she had a bite —Penny couldn't be more proud.

Nonna will haul out the magic wand if she hears that one. Though it's something I may have said if I was in her place.

Temper fired in Rafe's eyes as he stared at Savvy. "Don't be smart with me," he barked. "Do not give your security a hard time, or I will send some of the *extended la Famiglia* to babysit your every move. You are *not* an agent."

"Thanks for the reminder, yet again. Keep your goons and wise guys in New York. If you don't mind, I need to call my shopper."

I hope she means at Luxurious Department stores and not her friend Lexi.

Lexi was one of Savannah's friends since she was at her private boarding school. Some in the agent world believed Lexi was the world-renowned hacker *The Shopper.*

Penny's heart again skipped, this time from sadness. As Savannah's angered steps marched down the hall, she started rattling in French a hundred miles a minute.

And she didn't call the department store; she called the hacker.

Savannah not becoming an agent was a sensitive subject. Especially since her sweet younger cousin rivaled Zio Lenny's best—both men and women. She turned to her brother. "Why do you do that?"

"Do what?" Rafe inquired as if he literally had zero clue or cared how upset Savvy had been when she left the room.

"Come down so hard on her and make her feel like she's not good enough," Penny snapped.

Mac and Javier exchanged an unreadable look.

"She's the baby," Rafe retorted with a flare of nostrils and his end-of-subject tone.

Three simple words. However, Penny already could imagine the words that followed. She'd overheard them spoken too many times to count.

Silence stretched, and Javier cleared his throat.

"Mac and I will leave you two to catch up and check on Savannah," he flashed Penny a killer grin. "At least I don't have to worry about you trying to escape."

"She wouldn't dream of it," Rafe barked and rested his attention on Penny. "Would you?"

She loved her brother dearly, but sometimes there were times when she just wanted to punch him in his handsome face very hard. "Nope."

Both Javier and Mac exchanged another look and exited the room. However, she saw the questions in their eyes.

Penny sighed and glanced at her brother. "Thank you for coming."

"Of course," he whispered. Sadness worked over his features. "Do you think I'm too hard on Savvy?"

"Definitely," she admitted and thought of their cousin. "She isn't as weak as you make her out to be."

"But she isn't an agent," Rafe reaffirmed. "She's the baby. Now tell me, what's going on?"

Part of Penny shut down. She couldn't and wouldn't tell him what she'd been working on. However, he probably already knew. Despite being a doctor, her brother was a capo for la Famiglia. "I was following some arms dealers, and they got in a war with a drug dealer, and I getting shot was collateral damage."

Rafe shook his head. Obviously unhappy. "You

say this and make me worry twice as much about you and grateful every day that Savvy isn't an agent."

"Do you want me to come home?" Penny asked because she might as well face a firing squad if that was the case. Instead of bullets, questions would be fired at her until she was exhausted and wanted it to stop.

"You shouldn't fly, and I don't want you on anyone's radar. This cabin is remote; it is actually a lovely mountain area." Rafe crossed over to the monitor and removed the tape and finger reader connected to the monitor. Then turned the machine off.

He shoved a hand through his hair. "How much does Savvy know?"

"I don't know. Savannah is the creator of the bio-weapon, so maybe a lot. I haven't had time to talk to her," Penny responded, relieved to no longer be attached to the monitor. The thing was worse than a polygraph.

At least every time she made eye contact with Javier.

"Not about that, but you've been vaccinated. Just in case you were in contact and have had no adverse effects," Penny's brother replied and glanced to the empty threshold. "I mean about other stuff.

Other stuff, is that what we're calling it now?

Penny sighed as the weight of the world settled across her shoulders. "You mean family stuff?"

Her brother met her gaze and offered a weak smile.

Again she sighed. How honest should she be?

"I don't think she knows more than she should," Penny answered, then thought about Lexi. She should say something. If rumors were true. It was better her brother was forewarned. "I talked to Logan a while ago, and he knows Savannah knows nothing about the bits he remembers of anything and promises he won't bring it up. Thankfully they're close. Mac and Logan went to Harvard together. Zio Carlo approves of her with Mac."

"He seems decent, even if he didn't follow through and become a doctor or ask permission to marry her," he admonished.

This might not be an issue if the family wasn't so archaic. But why would my brother and the others pull their heads out of their asses after all this time? And now for me to drop the bomb.

"Savannah has a friend she went to Joan of Arc with," Penny began. She wanted to scream, *don't kill the messenger,* but refrained. Instead, Penny proceeded with caution—sort of. There was no easy way to say the words she was about to utter.

"What about her?" Rafe demanded. Patience was not her older brother's best trait.

"Lexi is a sweetheart, but some believe she's a

hacker and a good one in my world. All it takes is Savannah asking too many questions and reaching out to Lexi for answers. That's who she called when she stormed out of the room. Lexi is part of the French Connection, what Savvy and her friends call the friendship they formed when they were at Joan of Arc."

Rafe blinked in disbelief, then inhaled a breath. "Should I increase cyber security?"

If rumors are true, nothing will help.

"Maybe across all enterprises and let the others know," she offered.

"Fair enough. How are you feeling other than that?" Rafe asked, but she could see a new line on his forehead.

"Good, I had some messed up dreams," she confessed. Even now, blinks of images flickered through her mind like a cut film.

Rafe nodded. "That is very normal considering how much blood you'd lost. Thankfully there was some of Savannah's on standby, which Mac and I administered when we got here and while we operated." His face turned even more solemn. "Now I know why, knowing her situation was critical and possible kidnapping threats."

Penny thought of her dreams and started to doubt. "I guess I really am a Lucky Penny," she teased, but grief started to pinch her heart. She knew firsthand the kidnapping attempts were not just a possibility but a reality.

Suddenly Penny understood Savannah a little bit more and wondered.

What if my crazy-ass dreams aren't dreamed at all?

Could she have escaped the warehouse and ended up here because of ghosts?

She wasn't sure, but something inside told Penny the answer was yes.

CHAPTER 8

JAVIER WAS DISAPPOINTED to see Mac and Savvy leave and admitted he experienced minor relief to have Rafael Moretti on his way and out of Montana. He was also relieved that Hank or Chuck hadn't shown up while the group had been here. Javier wasn't up for the explanation. Then again, he knew Chuck and Lennox were friends.

Which reminded Javier why he was there.

Penelope.

Glancing at the clock on the microwave, he knew Penny would need her painkillers and antibiotics. Javier walked down the hall and looked into the room. She met his gaze and smiled at him, but the smile fell short of reaching her eyes.

"You're awake," he greeted.

"I am and starting to get hungry," she replied.

Her color was much better, and Javier studied the beauty before him. "Please, tell me they're gone."

Sighing, Javier nodded. "Yeah."

"My brother can be exhausting," she answered as if reading his mind. "I think I told you he was a headache; maybe I dreamed it," she stated, then furrowed her brow as if trying to recall.

"You did," Javier assured her and stepped into the room. "How are you doing?"

"Physically better, it's not like I haven't been shot before. Just never this bad," Penny revealed quietly and appeared lost in thought.

"You and your cousin share the same expression when something bothers you. My guess it's a Pierce trait," Javier began.

He had her there.

"Yeah," she admitted, and she patted the edge of the bed and nodded. "Will you keep me company for a bit?"

Javier couldn't control his grin. "Of course." He stepped over to the bed, reached for the pillows, and then repositioned her with care, so she was more upright.

"Better, thank you," she told him. "I'm sorry about my family. We're a bit dysfunctional."

Dysfunctional? That was one way of putting it. You're the fucking mob!

"Your monitor double beeped when Savannah

got upset, and your expression revealed sorrow," Javier carefully stated.

"Savannah wanted to be an agent more than anything, but her father wouldn't permit it. None of the family would." She glanced down at the blanket where her fingers touched the yarn ties of the quilt on her bed. "She was heartbroken, but it didn't matter. She's a scientific genius and finished her bachelor's degree before she graduated high school; she is a scientific prodigy and super smart."

Javier nodded in agreement. "She is, and I get why Mac and Rafe call her *Sugar,* even if they say it in two different languages."

"Yeah, she can be, and she's thoughtful," Penny agreed with a weak smile. "My Parent's had Rafe, then me, and Zio Lenny and his wife didn't have any. Then came Savannah. Shortly after that, I no longer had an aunt, Savvy didn't have a mother, or Zio Lenny, a wife. Another man lost all his children and two granddaughters. I don't think anyone recovered."

Javier's heart tightened, and he felt like she had confessed trade secrets—in some ways, she had. Her family was the mafia, and she was letting him in. "Why did you tell me this?"

Penny smiled, and this time, it reached her doe-like dark eyes. "Because I thought you needed to know, a free pass into my messed-up world. No one would have admitted the truth to my brother about how severe the threat was to our cousin. Especially since it dealt with classified information."

Yeah, and there is no guarantee hell won't be paid yet for that.

"I have younger female cousins. One of them is an only child—like Savannah. So I understand why your brother is overprotective." Javier admitted. "It's about trust, and as he says la famiglia prima di tutto."

"Family comes first," Penny repeated. "It means a lot in my family. We live by it, or so I thought," her last words came out in a sad whisper. "Now, I'm not so sure."

"Rafael is tough because he cares. I told Savvy the same thing, which was met with eye-rolling and her muttering French profanities," Javier assured.

There were so many things Javier wanted to ask her but didn't know where to begin. "I made my Abuela's asopao de pollo with rice. Your brother said clear liquids but figured you'd want something a little heartier than gelatin and broth."

"I think gelatin, and I include all of its funky and fun fruit flavors in this statement, is of the devil, and salads involving it, direct leftovers from his ass," Penny explained horrifiedly. "My brother knows I don't like that jiggly gross...eww."

Javier threw his head back and laughed. "I couldn't agree more, and there is none in the cabin. The asopao de pollo will still be light on your stomach. My mom and Abuela used to make it when one of us was sick."

Her beautiful face became bright. "Is that what I'm smelling? I didn't know you could cook. I think the aroma may have contributed to my current hunger. I don't know when the last time I ate was or how long I've been here."

Javier chuckled. "My brothers and cousins all know how to cook, as do I—including Agent Carter."

Penny's face became thoughtful. "I think my Zio Lenny has a pet by that name. In holding up a corner of the house, Agent Evan Darnell, he and his partner are usually kicking around the mansion. I was half tempted to bring dog treats the last time I visited."

Javier couldn't help but laugh. "Both are good agents, and I think they're more for Savannah's benefit. I can vouch for both men when she ran into trouble a few months back. They guarded her with their lives."

"Have you eaten yet?" Penny inquired.

"No, I haven't. I thought I'd see if you were hungry and make sure you take your meds," Javier answered.

She nodded her head and smiled. "Thank you for everything."

"You're welcome," Javier replied and stood. "I'll be back," he assured her and stepped toward the door. His head still processed everything she'd told him. He glanced back. "By the way, has anyone ever told you that you talk in your sleep?"

A strange expression crossed Penny's face. "No." She glanced down at the quilt yarn ties and then at Javier. "Do I even want to know what I said?"

"I don't think so because it's just going to have me ask questions," Javier admitted honestly.

Penny tilted her head. "And by not telling me, doesn't make you have the same questions?"

Javier lifted his brows. "Oh, I still have them, but I also know how mean Savannah can get when she's hungry, so I thought I'd offer to feed you first."

Penny broke into the most brilliant grin and then giggled. Immediately she winced, and her hand went to her side. "You are definitely more than a gorgeous face; you're a smart man."

He wasn't sure how to respond. Javier walked out of the room and wondered if Penny was as attracted to him as he was to her.

It didn't matter because whether she was or not, he couldn't get involved with Penelope Moretti. He had to protect her, and her uncle was Lennox Peirce.

Of course, there was also the fact that even though she was a CIA foreign operative, her brother was the mob.

And people wonder why I don't date.

CHAPTER 9

PENNY COULDN'T REMEMBER the last time she had a home-cooked meal. Six, maybe seven months ago. Possibly longer. Her Nonna was going to have her ass because the more she thought about it, the number was closer to eight months ago. She knew a lot her brother wanted to say and ask but had refrained since they were among people he didn't know, and the one he did know shouldn't be present for such discussions.

That person Savannah.

"Are you feeling okay?" Javier asked with concern. "Nauseous?"

She shook her head. "No, I'm surprisingly good. That was delicious. Thank you, I'm sorry I didn't eat more."

Javier cast her a warm smile, and her heart skipped a beat. Thankfully the vital monitor left with her brother and cousin, so no one else could witness the effect her sexy bodyguard had on her.

"I'm happy you're eating and are keeping it down," he admitted.

"I owe you a dinner. My Nonna taught me to cook well. She even made sure Rafe and my cousins could cook, told them it wasn't their wives' jobs to feed them; the first rule of survival was being able to feed themselves."

The former Navy SEAL grinned. "That sounds similar to what my mother said, and my oldest brother encountered a cuff to the back of his head when he got smart-mouthed," Javier grinned. "That night was his first cooking lesson because my Abuela said she would make him figure it out for himself, but she was afraid he'd burn the kitchen down."

Penny giggled, then put a hand to her side. "Sounds like what happened with my cousin Nicky when he informed Nonna he had no intentions of ever getting married."

Javier pursed his lips. "I'd never dream of making a comment like that in front of Abuela. I like my teeth in my mouth and not popping out between my lips from a cuff to the back of the head, which resembles a decapitation."

Again she laughed and pressed her hand to her side. "Nicky has no fear. He's a lawyer," she sighed and debated.

Javier studied her, and she lifted her gaze. "My guess personal injury or wrongful termination isn't his practice area."

Penny shook her head. "Not as a lawyer, but considering he's a mob defense attorney, personal injury and wrongful termination tend to come up, but not in the same context."

"My guess he's part of *la familglia*," Javier stated with a sigh.

"Yes," she admitted. "Does it bother you who my family is?" Penny asked as images of her dreams played like a broken movie, only missing pieces.

Big pieces.

"I thought it would bother me more," he replied honestly. "Savannah said something last night, and it kind of stuck with me, and I thought on it."

Penny was curious and nervous. Inwardly, she prayed it wasn't something to do with the family. "What did she say?" Her heart started to beat faster, and a small amount of fear prickled at her.

"Í asked how her father got the job working for the government, with rumored mob ties," Javier began, and a thoughtful expression worked over his face. "Savvy said over the last year and a half, she learned that the supposed good guys can be the worst of people, and even bad guys can have a heart and do good things. Even though she created the bioweapon accidentally, it eats at her."

Penny's heart hurt a bit, and tears filled her

eyes. Never did she cry. "It would; my cousin is sweet. She wouldn't do something to hurt people."

"I watched her kill Serpentine without hesitation as well as Agent Larson," he stated quietly. "Both times, she did it protecting those she loved."

She'd heard rumors through the grapevine. Penny knew if her family found out, they'd lock Savannah in a lab and never let her out.

"Hey, are you okay?" Javier inquired, and she looked into his dark eyes through thick black lashes.

"No," she confessed.

His strong hand reached out and gently curled around her fingers. "You're going to be okay." The feel of his hand on hers comforted her. She'd been around gorgeous men, agents of all sorts, and men with more money and looks than brains.

Yet there was something about Javier. Something special. She'd meant what she had said; he was gorgeous and intelligent. True, Penny had been through miserable and deadly situations. However, this time, things hadn't gone her way. She glanced at Javier and wished they could have met under different circumstances.

"Let me put the dishes in the kitchen," Javier told her and lifted the bed tray off the bed, which had their dirty bowls from dinner, "I'll be right back."

Javier left the room, and Penny looked around

as if seeing it for the first time. The place was neat, and she thought of her cousin Giovani, who was always meticulous. She could be that way. Careful, cautious, and leaving no evidence.

I left a blood trail.

Fear pricked at her wondering if anyone had seen her get in the vehicle in the alley. She is sure the men who rescued her had been cautious to a fault. One as meticulous as her cousin—he certainly didn't get the trait from a stranger.

Or did he?

Again clips of memories flashed through her mind like a bad commercial. Some from before her family crumbled, her laugh that of a small child. Only she didn't have pain in her side. Hell, her appendix was removed the same time they removed her tonsils a few months before her first mission with the CIA.

She knew it wasn't that.

Something isn't right. Why did I hallucinate? What if it wasn't a hallucination?

Nausea kicked her stomach, leaned her head back, closed her eyes, tried to inhale a deep breath, and enjoyed the quiet.

Silence. It wasn't quiet. It was silent.

There was no sound from the kitchen, nothing in the evening air around the cabin stirred. If Javier washed the dishes by hand, she knew from earlier she would hear the water running. She would've listened to the door open and close on the appliance if there was a dishwasher.

So much for still being lucky.

Every muscle in her body tensed, and every nerve went on alert.

She glanced around the room and missed her gun. This was Javier's place, a former Navy SEAL, and those people were more prepared than a Boy Scout group. Penny slid her hand under the bed.

Nothing.

Moving her body irritated her side. However, just sitting in the bed made her a sitting duck. She lifted her hand and felt behind the headboard. Her lashes closed as her fingers curled around the grip of the handle. Penny slid the gun out and knew this could be bad for her injury. She was positive Mac and her brother would have done an excellent job sewing her back up.

Part of her wanted to call out for Javier, but she would have heard the body hit the ground if he had been knocked out. Javier was a big guy.

And a distraction.

Every second that ticked by in the quiet reaffirmed her suspicion something was wrong. She threw the blankets back, moved her leg, then tried to move her left one and sunk her teeth into her tongue. Her side hurt, but not nearly as bad as before, and she got both feet on the floor. Penny was glad she had eaten. If she hadn't, when she stood, she wouldn't have the strength to stay that way.

Penny raised herself and came to a standing position. Her knees felt weird, but she knew the situation was critical. She stepped toward the threshold of the room and glanced in the hall. Her movement was slower than expected, and her side throbbed slightly, but she'd be fine.

Behind her was the back door with a bolt another room on her side of the hall. What she guessed was a third bedroom next to the bathroom across from her.

Silence.

She crossed the threshold into the hall and from the other end of a cool breeze. The front door was open. Penny kept her back to the wall and was already feeling light-headed. When she reached the end of the hall, she glanced into the living room.

Empty.

Where the hell is Javier?

She eased away from the wall, and she slightly swayed. Penny stepped into the kitchen area with her arms extended. The pain in her side ached in displeasure, and her legs felt weak. Two guns firing echoed from outside toward the back of the house. A strange voice called out in anger, in a language similar to Russian—but not. Another shot, only from a different gun, then quiet.

Heavy stomps moved quickly through the trees

and shrubs on the outside wall, and she wondered if it was a bear from the movement. Weighted steps clunked up the porch steps, and Penny knew it was shoot or die. Adrenaline fired through her blood, and she knew she had to stay standing to make a kill shot if needed.

Javier was a former SEAL, trained to be stealth would be his advantage in this situation, so she knew it wasn't him. She glanced to the safety of the semi-automatic to ensure it was off. In a slight pivot and turn, she stepped to the edge of the kitchen she glanced around the corner.

Terror filled her heart as one of the men from the warehouse entered the cabin. He was large, bigger than most. Blood ran from his ear and stained his shirt. Penny guessed both ears bled by the clothing color because his nose spewed blood, but the most frightening part was the blood running down his face like tears from his eyes.

It was something out of a horror movie.

How is this guy still alive?

She stepped out and fired her gun twice. Both center chest. The freak show turned to her in a zombie state as another weapon fired, and the beast dropped forward without half a head. Penny met Javier's gaze from where he stood on the cabin's threshold.

Penny leaned against the wall as Javier hurried

over to her. "Are you okay?" he asked and smiled as he glanced at the gun in her hand.

"I found it in the second place I looked," she stated as she started to lose feeling in her legs.

Javier's strong arms wrapped around her to steady her. "You shouldn't have got out of bed," he rasped.

She could control her smile. "I'm an operative, remember, and this was better than being a sitting duck on a bed."

He smiled, nodded, and her heart raced faster than when the giant zombie invaded. Javier darted a look to her lips, then met her gaze. Penny's lashes closed, and Javier's warm breath teased her mouth seconds before he lightly kissed her lips; then, it ended as fast as it began.

Penny blinked up into his gaze. "Despite the dead beast on the floor and another one outside, why did you…."

"I'm sorry," Javier apologized. "I wanted to do that before your brother kills me."

"I was going to say stop," Penny clarified.

Javier reached to his side and removed his satellite phone. "Mac, it's Rodrigues. I need you to turn that jet around, now!"

Now I understood what he meant. Maybe Rafe won't kill Javier.

Her gaze fell on the dead body filling the floor between the door and the dining table. Even if Rafe didn't kill him. There was nothing good that could come of this.

Penny rested against Javier's shoulder and savored the feel of being in his arms.

Something tells me I shouldn't fly is about to be changed to get your ass on that jet.

At least, she hoped not. If so, Javier was going with her, whether people liked it or not.

That included Penny's brother.

CHAPTER 10

Javier walked into the room Penny had been in and gently placed her down on the bed. However, her arms stayed around his neck. "I don't want you to leave me," she whispered.

"I don't want to leave you either, but I know you'll be okay here, and I won't be long. The sound of a truck echoed down the road. He fully expected to see Chuck or Hank's vehicles, only it wasn't their vehicles.

"What the hell?" It was the moving truck from earlier. He didn't understand.

Mac jumped out of the driver's side and Rafael out of the other.

Where the hell is Savannah?

The two men stepped around to the back of the truck and lifted the back door. Lewis and Cowboy jumped out of the back of the vehicle. Cowboy then turned and lifted Savannah out.

He exhaled a breath as the men grabbed equipment. Savannah gloved up and put on a mask. She turned and removed a camera with the forensic lens and put it over her neck. As Savannah turned, Javier spotted the gun tucked into the waist of her jeans. She glanced up at him but didn't say anything. There was an emotion in her eyes he couldn't identify.

Savannah walked into the house and glanced around. "Where's Penny?"

"Penny's in the room," Javier answered. The dark circles under Savannah's eyes weren't hard to miss, even under the dim lights of the cabin. "How'd you get back here so fast and with extra help?"

The four men approached with cases.

"We hadn't taken off yet," Savannah stated with a hint of temper. She looked at the dead body on the floor. Not a stitch of emotion reflected on her face. The four men entered the room, and Savannah shot them a scowl. She snapped some photos. "I'll be with Penny," she informed and walked down the hallway slowly, snapping a few more pictures.

"Why weren't you the air?" Javier asked his three friends and Penny's brother. "And how did Lewis and Cowboy get here?'

"Lewis and I flew out with Savannah since Mac was off to retrieve Rafe," Cowboy explained.

"Does Lennox have any idea where you two are?' Javier asked with surprise bouncing his attention between Lewis and Cowboy.

"No," Lewis replied. "However, I've hung out at the mansion long enough to know when Savannah is up to no good. So when Cowboy and I tailed her to the jet, we climbed aboard to keep the lovely scientist from getting into trouble."

"Why didn't you come the first time?" Javier asked.

His friends exchanged a look.

Son of a bitch, why do I suspect I will hate this?

"They were busy stealing dead bodies," Rafael answered. He closed the distance to where Javier stood. "What happened with my sister?"

"We finished eating, and I came out with the bowls, still on the counter as you can see, and I heard voices," Javier explained. "I snuck around and killed one at the back of the house. I came in as Penny was out of bed and had fired off two shots. I put a bullet in his head, he fell forward, then I helped Penny back into the room, and here you all are."

Rafael turned to Cowboy. "Instincts like none other?"

Cowboy met the other man's gaze. Something

silent transferred between the two. "Prometto," he responded in Italian.

I promise.

Javier glanced at Mac and Lewis, who exchanged unrevealing expressions. "What did I miss?"

"After I left to meet Rafael, Savannah called the CDC telling them she wanted the report from Bozeman," Mac explained. He shook his head. "Hazmat in Bozeman knew nothing about it. There was no paperwork; the last incident was when they busted up a meth lab four months ago."

"No," Javier wracked his brain and remembered the night and the relentless rain. "Hazmat was there when we pulled up at the warehouse."

"Oh yeah, there were people dressed as Hazmat when we arrived, and they were gone in record time," Lewis informed. "It explains why the room was supposedly cleared, yet we found chemicals."

Savannah walked down the hallway with the evidence bag and the gun inside.

"I took swabs of Penny's hands. She has tested positive for gunpowder residue, consistent with a semi-automatic." She placed a brown bag down. And dropped the clear plastic bags with the gun and magazine inside. Savannah stepped around the bag and clicked pictures of the casings lying on the ground by the kitchen entrance.

Something was wrong. Savannah was unusually quiet.

She turned to Javier. "Where is the other body?"

"Around back," he debated his words. "He's been infected."

Savannah met his gaze. "I figured. Maybe you boys can whip out your dicks and determine who's in charge, but I'm leaving in twenty minutes with or without you. So I'll leave you all to come up with a fucking clue in the meantime."

"Savvy!" Rafael barked. "Language!"

"Sorry, capos for the Giordano crime family can't take the lead, so at least that's one trauma I can avoid by keeping your protruding parts in your pants," she replied.

"Savannah!" Cowboy called and looked at her. His cowboy boots shifted, and he placed a hand on his hip. She turned and looked at Javier's long-time friend. "Cut Rafe some slack," he boomed.

She never said a word and instead walked over to the body, taking up a great deal of space between the door and the dining table. Savannah approached like a pro and took the photos.

No one spoke.

Mac glanced at Javier. "Show us where the other body is. We'll get it bagged. We can process it back at the compound."

"Rafe, go with them. I'll stay with Lewis and help Savannah with this body," Cowboy assured.

Javier crossed the floor to the threshold and led Mac and Rafael out the door. Rafael paused and turned to Savannah. "Do you hate me because of the family's reputation?"

She looked up over her camera.

"No, I don't hate you at all," she responded without emotion in her tone. "I can't hate you because I don't know you. It's nice that I've spent the last few days with you. However, it doesn't make up for the Christmas, Thanksgiving, or Easter, not having you come to visit, or being at a single birthday party while I was growing up. It wouldn't have mattered what people said about you or the family. It just would have been nice to have a family."

Cowboy turned his back, so he faced Lewis. Javier imagined it was to hide his emotions. Rafael continued out the door, but grief etched in his face. He didn't speak, but he and Mac followed Javier to the back of the house. Sure enough, the body was still there.

"His gun is still in his hand," Mac noted.

"I knew he was dead. He wasn't going anywhere," Javier stated. "I didn't want Penny unattended."

"Appreciated," Rafael told him, then met his gaze. "I mean that. My family and I thank you."

Javier nodded as Rafael flashed his light over the body. "There is a hole close to his head where he ripped out a tree."

"Did you say a tree?" Rafael ran his light up against the trees. "That isn't possible."

"He got roots and all," Javier explained. "Fight night on the mountain."

Rafael ran the light and then stopped on the face. His nose and eyes had leaked blood down his face. A clear distinction between that and the bullet that penetrated the forehead. "He shows signs of Ebola."

"It was root RNA string in the bioweapon," Mac informed. "Something went wrong when Savannah introduced the Malaria string, and it came in contact."

Rafe put on a mask and pulled on his gloves. "Got enough pictures?' he asked Mac.

"That should do it," Mac called and removed a body bag from his case. Javier reached out and grabbed the other end.

"Javier, how long has it been since you shot him?" Confusion lingered over Dr. Moretti's words

"About forty minutes maybe less," He changed a look with Mac, then both looked to Rafael. "Why?"

"Pass me a thermometer, please." Rafael waved his light down the body and then ripped open the shirt. He sliced the dead body as Mac passed him a thermometer and stuck it in the incision.

Rafael held the thermometer and glanced at his

watch. He studied the thermometer. "Mac, this thing works, right?"

Mac stepped next to him and looked. "Everything goes through a check. These cases were repacked before I left to see you." He looked at the device still in the dead man's body. "That's not possible, but it's right."

"Speak to me, guys," Javier demanded.

"According to this, this guy has been deceased for over eight hours," Rafael informed. He removed the thermometer, passed it to Mac, then reached for the arm with the gun in its hand and pulled it.

Nothing.

Rafael and Mac looked at each other. Rafael flipped the flashlight around and cracked it against the knuckles. The cracking of bones filled the night air. "What the hell?" Javier asked.

"He's in full rigor mortis," Rafael breathed. "This isn't normal."

"Nope," Mac agreed. "But it coincides with the body temperature."

"Let's get this body bagged and get the hell out of here," Mac whispered.

Rafael made notes and looked up. "I like that idea." He scanned the light up to the eyes. "What are the chances you guys have an ophthalmoscope?"

"Yep," Javier grabbed the one for the kit and

passed it to Rafael. "One too many jobs working with Mac."

Rafael turned it on, examined the eyes, then passed the light to Mac, who leaned in and looked at both eyes. "I don't understand. His eyes look more like affixation than consistent with a gunshot."

"I agree," Mac concurred as he turned off the light, passed it to Javier, and nodded. "Help me with this," he said to Javier as Rafael scribbled more notes.

"I'll help Mac," Rafael volunteered. "Please check on Penny and Savvy."

Javier nodded and walked back around the house.

Penny was in Cowboy's arms, wrapped in the quilt on her bed. "Are you okay?" Javier asked in worry and stepped over to his friend, holding the wounded agent.

"I'm fine," Penny stated quietly. "I love this blanket, and I know if I get a chill, we'll have to listen to Rafe bitch."

Javier smiled at Penny. "My Abuela made that for me when I returned from my first deployment."

Her fingers curled around the blanket a little tighter, pulling it around her. "I'll take care of it."

His heart beat faster, and the thought of their brief kiss flashed through his mind. "I know you will." In truth, seeing her wrapped in that blanket affected him to the root of his being. Everything seemed more personal.

If she's in my blanket, does that make her mine?

"My nonna and aunts made one for all the grandkids," Penny began. "Mine is still on my bed back in New York."

"I still have mine," Cowboy admitted. "It's my favorite blanket when I get home off missions and fall asleep on the sofa."

"I'll be outside with the evidence," Savannah stated and hurried out the door.

It wasn't so much the words. It was the tone of voice that changed the air in the room.

Sorrow.

"I shouldn't have said anything," Penny whispered.

Cowboy sighed, increasing his hold on Penny. "I'm just as much to blame."

Javier glanced to Lewis, who nodded and walked out after Savannah.

Tears filled Penny's eyes. "I'm sorry," she sobbed.

His heart ached. Javier quickly brushed her tears away gently with a finger. "No need to apologize. Families can be tough," he reassured.

Penny cast him a watery smile; more than anything, he wanted to remove her from Cowboy's arms and hold her. The look in the other man's eyes revealed his grief. Javier had no idea what the hell was going on. However, he suspected the Pierce and Moretti problems were more extensive than most families.

The question was, why? Other than the whole mob thing.

CHAPTER 11

PENNY GLANCED across the limousine at her cousin Savannah as she withdrew her phone. "Prepare the protection team," she spoke in fluent French.

The limousine passed through the gates of the Pierce compound, and Penny's stomach started to ache as she glanced out one of the blackened windows. "You are so busted zio is waiting on the threshold," she leaned against Javier's muscular shoulder and pulled the blanket around her. The one his Abuela had made, she one cherished as much as being in the former Navy SEAL's arms.

Penny felt safe, despite the danger. She hadn't felt that way in years.

She glanced to Rafael, who hadn't spoken a word. Then again, neither did Savvy. She had remained unreadable since she'd walked out of the cabin back in Montana.

Closing her eyes, Penny fought back the tears. She never realized how sad her cousin was, but after the last few days, she understood more than anyone.

"Everyone, take positions. Witness on the move," Savannah stated into her phone as men exited the rear vehicle. "Be sure she gets in the house," she ordered of Javier. "Please."

"Of course," Javier whispered.

"Mac, Cowboy, move once Rafael and I clear the steps," Savannah stated, and the limousine door opened. Then the passenger side. Both Penny's cousin and brother exited the vehicle with guns drawn. There was something in Savannah's walk she'd never noticed before.

The way of the huntress, not the prey.

"She's smarter than us," Penny whispered quietly.

Cowboy's expression turned grave. "You're tired. She's not an agent, remember?"

"That's what makes this scarier," Penny replied. "Javier will take me in. He was assigned to my security detail."

Cowboy nodded, then exchanged a look with Mac, who was far from impressed. If anyone had insight into her cousin, it would be Mac. However, despite working with him years before, now she undoubtedly knew his loyalty was to her cousin.

"What does she know?" Penny asked Mac.

The supervisory agent shook his head. "I don't know. I've been wondering since your brother, and I landed in Bozeman. Maybe she's just tired, or the fact she is about to face the music."

"You mean Zio Lenny," Penny supplied.

"That's who he means," Javier assured, then turned to Mac and Cowboy. "Go, I'll take Penny."

Both men removed their guns, flipped the safety off, and exited the vehicle. But instead of entering the house, they took positions giving the limousine extra coverage.

"Don't misread your cousin," Javier whispered. "She knows what she's doing."

Penny tilted her head up and met his gaze. "That's what terrifies me."

Javier kissed the top of her head. "Trust me, *Mi Reina*."

My queen. Could he be any sweeter?

Javier flashed Penny a smile. "You ready?"

"Zio is going to be upset; I haven't seen him in eight or nine months," she admitted.

A thoughtful expression worked across Javier's handsome face. "Whatever happens inside, know your uncle was scared and worried. He loves you, Penny, despite whatever family troubles have transpired."

Javier made a good point, and she nodded. He pulled her into his lap, swung his powerful legs out of the limousine, and stood, not once losing his grip on her. In fast-paced strides, Javier crossed the drive, hurried up the steps, and then crossed the threshold to the large Pierce mansion.

"Penny, thank god!" her Zio greeted. He turned to Javier. "Thank you, but she shouldn't have flown."

Javier eased Penny down, and her feet touched the ground. He didn't let go of her until she demonstrated stability.

The others entered the house, and the armed men who had been in the vehicle behind faded into the darkness. No doubt they were going to do a perimeter and grounds check. Her Zio turned and met Rafe's gaze. "Do I even want to know how you got involved?"

"Savannah and Mac reached out to me, and Mac assisted me in removing the bullet from inside her," Rafe replied and darted a glance to Savannah.

He then met their uncle's gaze—there was no mistake which side of the family her brother got his blue eyes from. They were the exact shade of their Zio and their mother. "It's good to see you." He stepped forward and embraced the man in a hug. A slow smile worked across Cowboy's face. Her Zio Lenny then turned and hugged Penny. "How are you feeling?'

"Rafe knocked me out, so the pain on the jet wouldn't bother me as bad. It did cause some bleeding from the pressure, but not as bad as they expected. I heal relatively quickly," she admitted. "Thankfully, they hadn't left Montana when Javier's cabin was attacked."

"Yes, imagine my surprise to discover there was a team there." He then turned to Savannah. "Since I didn't give orders."

Savannah straightened up. "You forget yourself, it was need to know, and at the time, you didn't need to know. However, I'll let your agents brief you. I have to go to the morgue."

"For what?" Zio boomed.

"Five dead bodies." She hit the elevator button. "The two from the cabin on the attack on Penny and Javier, plus the three we liberated in Bozeman."

Her Zio Lenny blinked at her cousin. "You stole dead bodies?"

"I'm not comfortable with the word *stole*. I like to think of it as more a relocation program courtesy of the government," Savannah replied as the elevator doors opened.

"I'll help you," Mac told her and stepped toward the elevator. "No, I'm good. That's what dad's new recruits are for." She then glanced at her dad. "Enjoy the family reunion," she added with a heavy dose of sarcasm as the doors closed.

She's not close to her dad. Why?

Something seemed off. Savannah was an only child, so she should have had all of his attention.

"That girl needs an attitude adjustment, more than another degree," Zio Lenny snapped.

What is it with the men in this family?

Penny blinked at her uncle. "Because of her instincts, I'm alive," she whispered. "She'd already reached out to Rafe before I asked Javier for my brother."

Despite her words, her Zio and brother both wore displeased expressions.

"What the hell were you men thinking?" her Zio demanded of the agents in the room. "My daughter doesn't have the authority to tell government agents what to do."

"Actually, she does; her security clearance warrants that if it involves a threat to national security, she can pull any government resource as needed," Mac informed. "Two bodies from the cabin have been exposed or have come in direct contact with Malebola."

"How?" the simple word fell off her zio's tongue.

Years of being with the CIA and a Moretti knew her Zio Lenny was telling the truth. I wasn't the single word question. It was the tone

"That's one of the many questions we need to find answers for," Javier stated.

"Initiating back up protocol basement, section A," an automated voice declared, and the screens in the hallway kicked on. "Bringing up audio," the computerized voice announced.

Penny glanced at the two flat screens and noticed a third larger one further down the hallway. “What the hell?”

“Savannah’s main lab is just down from the kitchen. However, the morgue and two other labs are in the basement,” Zio Lenny explained. “The system was installed when the threat on Savannah became critical, and there were dirty agents inside the compound here.”

She darted a look to her brother, who stared at their uncle with a seething glare. Yeah, dirty agents who could get to Savannah were probably the last thing Rafe needed to hear. Penny had no doubt the family would be briefed about this. By the look on Rafe’s face, he would spare nothing.

“Today, people, I want a shower and to stop smelling like a green paper pine tree hanging from a review mirror,” Savannah barked like a drill sergeant.

Snickers and expressions of amusement worked across the men’s faces—except her zio’s. Even Rafe had lifted his brows and wore a tiny smirk. A couple of the men who’d given protection detail walked in carrying a body. They continued with the others and brought in the fifth one near Savannah's table.

“Why is that one leaking?” Rafe asked and pointed to a body bag on the screen, the third one in.

"That one must have punctured a leak," one of the probationary agents called, then glanced at the floor "Where Savannah stood. "So is the one you're in front of."

"Move, get out of here," she ordered as she jumped up on an empty metal examination table, the spot she had been in seconds before filled with blood. Just then, one of the body bags bent and came to a seated position.

Penny's heart stopped.

"What the fuck?" Lewis gasped as he stared in shock at the screen.

This was terrible streaming.

Savannah jumped off the metal table in a parkour-like half turn as she pulled her gun and then shot the top of the body bag where the head would be. The body bag fell back flat onto the metal surface. "I said move," Savannah kicked the agent back with her hiker and hit the emergency button. As the glass doors shut, she shoved the agent want-to-be through. "Initiate irradiation," she barked as the camera shifted to a containment hallway on the other side of the morgue.

Savannah spun to the agent she had kicked back and threw him against the wall with her forearm to his throat. "The next time you're told to move, do it or prepare to die. That goes double for when you're in the field," she yelled, back in drill sergeant mode.

"That agent looks scared," Carter chuckled.

Savannah glanced down to the floor between her and the agent, then met the agent's gaze pinned to the wall. "You'll be cleaning that up," she told him in a no-BS tone.

Quiet chuckles echoed. Rafe's wasn't one of them. Instead, his gaze was fixed on the screen with a look of contempt.

Holly hell. The family would never believe this or that Savannah is not an agent.

She removed her arm from the agent's throat and stepped back. "Both of you strip off your clothes and get in the showers."

"What is going to happen to our clothes? I'm in a three-hundred dollar suit," the agent who had remained quiet until now voiced.

That would be the day one of the men in my family wore a three hundred-dollar suit. More like nine thousand.

"Bad news, you overpaid. In answer to your question, burned, however, if that piece of polyester means that much to you, I will ensure you get the proper paperwork for reimbursement," Savannah sneered in a condescending tone. "And please be advised burning your tie will be a mercy killing."

Penny sneered. They were a lot alike.

Savannah headed toward a locker room. The two agents exchanged looks. "The rumors are true about Dr. Pierce. Everyone says the scientist is a bitch," the one worried about his suit complained.

"I thought she was going to kill me," the one who had been pinned to the wall by Savannah's forearm stated. "She's killed agents before," he said as he and the other man walked into the locker room, and the screen went fuzzy.

"How do you know she's safe?" Penny asked, trying to piece so many things together in her head.

"Panic button in a locked area in the irradiation showers. She'll be okay." Mac assured.

"She sure as the hell better," Rafe seethed and glared at Zio Lenny.

Mac cleared his throat. "Rodrigues put Penny in the room next to Savannah's. There is a connecting door if needed. The room can be accessed from two sides."

"I'll deal with you all in a bit. First, I'd like a word with my nephew," Zio Lenny told the room.

"And I with you," Rafe assured in an eerie calm and a sardonic grin.

Oh hell, here we go. Let the war begin.

Javier turned to Penny. "Get ready," he warned and swooped her up. Her side hurt, but Penny knew the stairs would not be her best friend, especially since there were so many of them. She slipped her arms around Javier's neck, and he turned a corner, then walked down and opened a door. He placed her feet gently down on the floor.

"Thank you," she told him as he helped her to the bench in front of the bed.

He studied her. "Are you okay?" Concern in both his tone and the expression on his face was unmistakable.

"I'm not sure," Penny stated. "I'm trying to wrap my brain around things. Being here feels familiar and yet strange. I didn't realize things were so bad between Savvy and her dad."

She should have been with us.

"Pretty normal for the two of them," Javier sat on the bench next to her and smiled. "You'll be safe here. You need to recover."

Penny debated her following words. "I don't want you to leave me. Stay in here with me tonight?"

Hesitation worked its way across his gorgeous face. "I shouldn't." Silence stretched for a few seconds then he nodded. "Yeah."

True, this may not be wise, and people may disapprove, but Javier is what Penny needed more than anything. Maybe she should talk to him about what happened and about her crazy hallucinations.

Because deep down inside, Penny still wondered if they were real.

CHAPTER 12

JAVIER STUDIED THE BEAUTY. "I need to brief Lenny. Savannah will probably be up shortly and help get you settled." He stole a glance at her lips and lowered his head. Javier lifted a hand and gently placed it under her chin as her lashes fluttered closed. His mouth connected with hers. This time, he showed less resistance than he had at the cabin and deepened the kiss.

Penny's full lips parted in a soft gasp, inviting his tongue to enter and gently explore her mouth. Javier's groin tightened; he wanted to throw her back onto the bed more than anything. The thought created an imaginary bucket of ice and poured down around him.

He ended the kiss and eased back as her eyes opened. "I know I shouldn't have done that," he whispered. Wondering what the hell he was thinking.

Right. Javier wasn't.

"No, probably not," Penny answered, then a tiny smile curled across her delectable mouth. "But I wanted you too."

Despite a whole section in the policy and procedure manuals about not getting involved with witnesses, those undergoing criminal investigations, and those under protective services, Javier didn't care. "I've wanted to kiss you again since I first kissed you."

The smile on Penny's face brightened. "Well, then I hope you do so again."

Lord, the things I want to do to her.

How many missions? How many beautiful women had he been around?

Countless, yet he was acting like a newbie by kissing the boss's niece. Who was also a mob boss's granddaughter or goddaughter? Javier thought a moment. Maybe he needed a CT scan or an ass-whopping from the smart stick.

"I'll be back soon. I'm sure one of the guys is already outside the door," he assured and stood.

Penny smiled then nodded before Javier turned and walked to the open door. He closed it behind him.

"A word of advice," Mac said quietly, leaning

against the wall. "If you're going to kiss her, do it in a spot no one can witness it."

Javier's stomach lodged into his throat. "You saw that?"

"Yeah. Better me instead of Lenny or Rafael," he lightly joked.

Good point.

"You're falling for her," Mac voiced quietly, though the comment might have been a question.

"Yes," he replied as his chest tightened with a pang of guilt. "And I know that isn't wise or smart. I need to protect Penny and help you all figure out what the hell is going on with the Malebelo." He paused and thought a moment. "How is Savannah doing?"

Mac sighed heavily. "Blames herself every day for creating the weapon."

"It was an accident," Javier reminded.

"I know," Mac replied. "However she can be as stubborn as Penny, a family trait—not to mention we know how Lennox can be."

"There's that," Javier agreed.

"As far as falling for Penny, not giving in can be a bigger distraction than seeing what happens," Mac chuckled. "I know from first-hand experience."

True that.

Javier looked at him. "Please don't—"

"It's not mine to tell," Mac replied with a

charming grin. "Come on, and let's see if Cowboy has survived *la famiglia* interrogation."

Concern worked over Javier as the two men walked toward the stairs. "Do I even want to know?"

Defeat worked across his friend's face. "Lenny and Rafael weren't even in the office two minutes when Rafael went off on Lenny. Then Lenny yelled, and the next thing you know, the office door opens, and Lenny beckons Logan." He shook his head. "The look on Cowboy's face was between anger and defeat."

"You heard what Rafael said at the cabin. Logan is *la famiglia*," Javier reminded.

"Yeah," Mac answered thoughtfully. "What if it's personal, with Penny and Savannah?"

"What do you mean?" Javier asked and thought of the situation. "You mean with the Moretti's being part of the Giordano crime family?"

Mac shrugged as they walked down the stairs and past Lenny's office in silence.

"She should have been with the family," Rafael boomed.

"Savannah is my daughter. She belonged with me," Lenny yelled back. Temper and anger coated every word.

"She saved Penny. Tell me, what the hell were you doing other than sitting in this office pretending to be important?" Logan demanded.

Javier exchanged a look with Mac, and they walked into the kitchen, where Lewis sat with Darnell and Carter. "You look like you need a beer, Primo," his cousin Jared Carter told Javier and reached into the fridge.

He shook his head. "I can't. I'm on security detail."

"Not tonight," Darnell replied. "That's what I and Agent Carter and I are for. You are going to need sleep. Besides, the grounds are heavily guarded after the horror show in the morgue."

"She followed protocol to the letter," Javier stated. "If a corpse sat upright in the room I was in, I would have fired too."

"But could you have done it in a half turn flip, from a table with wheels?" Lewis asked.

Javier thought of Savannah shooting the corpse. The shot was precise. "Maybe, but I'm a former Navy SEAL. Why?"

"I don't know if I could have done what she did," Darnell replied. "Like you, maybe. She fired while in the flip the bullet hit the body as her feet hit the ground. I do know that she doesn't put up with crap. Most of the new recruits don't take her seriously.

"I blame Lenny," Jared replied, passing Javier a beer. "He doesn't take Savannah seriously."

"He's a fool," Rafael stated behind Javier and Mac. "Savvy should not be underestimated," he added quietly.

"Can we get you a beer?" Javier asked.

Rafael smiled weakly. "Please, call me Rafe. I think I'd prefer something much stronger than a beer. How is my sister?"

"Let me grab the good stuff," Mac assured. "My dad sent me a twenty-five-year-old bottle of scotch. I've been waiting for a reason to open it."

"Mac, I'm starting to warm up to you." Rafe placed a hand on Mac's shoulder. "Let's get one thing straight, now. One does not need a reason to open a bottle of scotch."

"Mac, I think you should totally take the man's advice," Javier laughed, "And sign me up for some of that."

"I seriously hope it's for printing classes, Rodrigues," Savannah started coming from the side stairwell dressed in pale pink scrubs. "Your penmanship is atrocious."

He couldn't help but snicker. Yeah, Lennox and others had bitched more than once over the legibility of his handwriting.

She entered the room with two evidence bags and papers in one hand and two packages of scrubs, a blue and mint set, which she passed to Rafe. "I thought these would do until you raid one of these guys' closets."

"Thank you," her cousin told her as he took the

scrubs. "And even more thanks for not grabbing me pink."

"The only pink ones around here are my size and would never fit you. If they did, I'd never eat another cookie, cupcake, or slice of cheesecake," Savannah told him.

"And the rest of us would have to deal with her," Javier chuckled. "She is much nicer after coffee and sugar."

Rafe looked as if he was about to comment but refrained. "What was the black liquid coming out of the bag?"

"You saw that?" Savvy asked.

"Security system kicked on," Lewis informed her quietly. "We saw the whole thing."

Savannah swallowed and nodded, then met her cousin's gaze. "Blood, and it was like dirty motor oil. The other bag that was leaking sat up."

"We saw that too," Javier told her quietly.

She placed one of the bags on the table. "My gun's magazine and bullets are in the bag. I need one of you to sign the chain of evidence and put it in my lab. I'm going to get Penny settled."

Javier took the bag from her, looked inside, and signed the form. "You're good to go."

"Also, I ordered pizza because the CDC will be locking the compound down." She turned to Rafael. "You might want to call the hospital and tell them you'll be delayed."

"I will, thank you." He dipped his brows. "What's wrong, Ciccio?"

"Something Penny said when I did the gun powder test on her hands. She said the gunman was bleeding from the eyes, ears, and nose and described him as a zombie. A double shot to the heart didn't kill him."

"I shot him in the head, close range from behind," Javier confirmed. "You saw the forehead shot on the one behind the cabin. I, too, had no luck with a double to the heart."

"That explains why the one in the cabin didn't have a front half of a head," Savannah explained. "You weren't here, but Mac, Lewis, Carter, and Darnell were when Executive Assistant Director Hodges convulsed in my dad's office from being infected. He was unresponsive."

Rafe turned to Mac. "Is that true?"

Mac nodded his head. "He had the same bleeding from eyes, ears, nose, and mouth. He was vomiting and convulsing. His body was going into shock. I held him down so Savannah could get a blood sample in hopes of finding a cure."

"I know those gunmen had advanced stages of Malebola. They shouldn't have been walking around trying to kill people, and I don't think dead men are supposed to sit up," Savannah sighed, shaking her head as if trying to come up with an answer. “They were in the cargo of the jet. It would have kept their bodies cool.”

“Cool enough,” Mac agreed and exchanged a look with Rafel, who nodded once concurring, but he too looked as if he were trying to solve a puzzle.

“Oh, and someone better get their ass out to the front gate. I ordered thirty-five pizzas,” Savannah told them with a mischievous grin. “Since we’re locking down for five days, I wanted to be prepared. I need someone to retrieve them. The Chinese food should be here then, so whoever goes for the food should bring a friend.”

“You better have gotten spring rolls,” Javier said with a grin.

“You know it,” Savvy replied. “I got the buffet pack, which normally feeds a group of fifty, but they are cutting off food service for the duration, so I figured why not? I can’t cook six meals daily for you and help care for Penny.”

“I’ll handle the abundance of food,” Javier assured her. “Lewis, Jared, come with me. Mac, get the scotch.”

“I’ll be with Penny,” Savannah told them and started down the hallway.

Lenny stepped out of the office. “Savannah, get your ass in here and start explaining.”

She turned and glared at her father. “You forget yourself. I’m not one of your ass-kissing agents. I will brief you when I complete processing the evidence. Right now, my cousin needs more than you're need-to-know."

"You scared the hell out of my new recruit," her father yelled.

Beside Javier, Rafe stiffened his back. He was having issues with how Lennox spoke to Savannah. Rafe could get in line.

"Well, your new recruit grows a pair or finds a job where he doesn't have to listen to orders," Savannah fired back.

"You have no right giving direction to my men."

"I do, actually, and if you don't believe me, you can call the head of the Centers for Disease Control and discuss it with him," she informed her father, not backing down.

Shock worked over Lenny's face. "Then stop scaring my men."

"No," she replied in pure temper, not backing down in the slightest. "Because that's what monsters do. They scare and kill people."

"Here we go again," Mac muttered, then exhaled a heavy sigh. None of the guys spoke as Savannah ran up the stairs.

"I'll deal with the rest of you later," Lennox boomed and slammed his office door.

Javier figured he would and exchanged a look with a pissed-off Rafe.

CHAPTER 13

THE CONNECTING door between the room Penny sat and Savannah's opened, and her cousin walked through with an arm full of things. "New satin pajamas and a robe to match," she told her and placed them on the bed. "I also grabbed some body wash, shampoo, and conditioner that don't smell woodsy, male musk, or like pine."

Penny couldn't help but laugh. "It's appreciated, but I probably shouldn't with the bandage over the stitches."

"Ah, yes, I thought of that too," she replied and hauled out plastic and surgical tape. Rumor is

Penny was excited about a hot shower. "I don't remember the last time I took a shower without a gun or knife nearby."

She hadn't moved from where she had sat with

Javier. Instead, she'd looked around the room, absorbing every detail. Classy, elegant and reminded her of home—undoubtedly, her mother had her hand in this. "The room is pretty."

"Your mom helped my dad with décor for the house and asked me what I wanted to see. I wasn't sure," she shrugged. "I told her I wanted it classy but comfortable. This room was always Melanie's favorite."

"I keep forgetting you went to school with Melanie McCormick at Joan of Arc. She's part of the French Connection."

Her cousin smiled and nodded as she set the basket of bath stuff in the bathroom. "She is indeed. I still talk often with the others. Kate sends me clothes all the time. She and her daughter still live in Paris. The pajamas and the robe are compliments of her."

Penny turned and noticed the tags. She glanced back at Savannah. "These are Fayette, only like the hottest, most exclusive designer in Europe."

"I have a lot of Fayette. Kate sends it to Melanie and me all the time, the robe and pajamas, please keep them. I've never worn them."

"Yeah, the tags still hanging on them tipped me off," Penny sighed and ran a hand over the silky smooth fabric on the robe sleeve. She couldn't help but smile. "I feel spoiled."

"Is that so bad?" Savannah asked. "Besides, I'm happy you're here."

I've missed her so much.

"They are locking down the compound," Savannah informed. "No one can leave for five days, so I want you comfortable. My closet is your closet, and the second drawer in the closet is unworn undergarments, all new and all Fayette."

"You realize when I leave, I'll take quite a few contents of the drawer with me."

Her cousin shrugged. "I hope you do."

Penny nodded, then realized the whole meaning of what Savannah was saying. "Where's Rafe?"

A strange expression worked across Savannah's face. "Downstairs, is something wrong?"

"He's stuck here?" Penny asked, and her heart started to race in a minor panic. "Here at the compound?"

Savannah nodded her head and studied Penny with concern. "Do you want me to go get him?"

"No," Penny tried to wrap her head around the situation. "He shouldn't be here."

Savannah pushed her hair back with the combing motion of her fingers. "Right, because my dad trains agents like you and the guys, and Rafe is a doctor and a capo for the mob."

"I don't know how Padrino will react with him being here," she confessed quietly. "I don't want Rafe in trouble."

"Does Padrino forget my aunt is your mother?" she asked, obviously upset.

Penny wanted to scream. Sometimes life was beyond cruel. "No, Ciccio, he never forgets," she assured Savannah. "One day, I'll explain. It's complicated," Penny thought of her Zio. Images of Quinn leaning over her flashed through her mind.

"Penny?" Savannah spoke, snapping her out of her memories of the hallucinations.

"I'm sorry," she apologized.

"Are you sure you're okay?" Savannah asked with furrowed brows of concern.

A knock came at the door. "Come in," Penny called.

The door opened, and Rafe poked his head in. "I just wanted to check on you," her brother replied. He glanced at the pajamas and robe on the bed. "Those are nice," Rafe whistled. "And expensive."

Penny giggled. "Not for Savannah. One of her friends, Kate, lives in Paris and always sends her clothes."

"Fayette? Wow, next girlfriend I get, I'll give you a call," her brother teased Savannah. He glanced around the room. "I swear mom decorated this place."

"She did," Penny and Savannah both commented simultaneously.

"So you're really here for the next five days?" Penny asked her brother.

"CDC shut the compound down, so everyone in the house is kind of stuck here. I admit I never saw this coming," Rafe admitted. "It won't be too bad," he darted a quick look at Savannah.

"Don't worry," Savannah assured and walked over to the open door. "If you swim in the meter pool outside and take advantage of the workout room, it will feel like less of a prison." She went to step over the threshold.

"Not so fast, and shut the door," Rafe ordered.

Surprising to Penny, Savannah listened and did what Rafe had asked. She turned and blinked at Rafe. "I don't want to argue."

"No, I just want to know what it was like growing up here," he asked out of curiosity.

"Fine, I guess. Dad had his life training agents, and I eventually went off to school, so it was okay, as normal as it could be. Lots of money, workaholic dad, I could hang out with friends and learn. Read the nerdiest books I wanted without anyone telling me to go outside and play instead. As I got older, I appreciated the eye candy of new recruits, but at first, I was too young, then I just stopped caring. They were all the same. I focused on science and eventually my Doctor of Medicine degree in pathology."

"You're so young," Penny shook her head and debated. "Are things always like that with your dad and you?"

"Oh, you mean strained," Savannah shrugged. "Tonight was average. We've had worse fights. He knew I would have gone after the agents on Serpentine's compound behind his back. He conceded more than he approved, but I knew by going and appeasing the crime lord, I'd buy the men time. Anyway, I'll leave you to talk."

Defeat worked across Rafe's face, and Penny wished she had some clue what he was thinking.

In the blink of an eye, Savannah was gone, and Penny sighed. "Is Padrino going to be mad?"

"Livid, but not so much with me," her brother responded and met Penny's gaze. "But I want to be here. You're in danger, and despite the smiles, I don't think Savannah's okay. Something is bothering her, I mean more than her father."

"You fought with Zio Lenny," Penny sighed and was glad guns didn't get involved. "At least you didn't kill each other."

Rafe shook his head. "I'm not like the rest of the family. I'm not forgiving."

Sadness rolled over Penny like a cold rain. "Our parents should have fought for custody of her."

"They were going to and were advised against it," Rafe confessed. "That's why mom always comes alone or with you. The restraining order only applies to the others and dad, but not to you, me, or mom. I stayed away, and I shouldn't have, but I didn't want the others to resent me." The animosity in his tone wasn't hard to miss as he ran his hand through his hair.

Penny hated the grief in his tone. "Why do you think they would?"

"Because I resent Logan when he briefly mentions her name. Vinnie often looks like he's been kicked in the stomach," Rafe admitted as raw emotions came to the surface. "This will sound crazy, but I'm glad to be here. As inconvenient as it is for my career, I think this will be okay. I'll have a bit of time with you and Savvy both. The agents you've worked with and the others are nice."

"Even Mac?" Penny asked.

Rafe tilted his head from side to side. "Yeah, but don't tell Savannah. I want her to sweat. I understand why he's one of Logan's best friends. He's a good guy, comes from money, and our cousin is his everything. Now that we have privacy, what's going on with you?"

I'm attracted to my bodyguard and dream of dead people.

Nope. Penny couldn't have that conversation with her brother just yet. "I'm okay. Still shaken and losing my mind, I now smell Chinese food," Penny laughed.

"Not crazy; Savannah made the preemptive order before they locked down the compound and ordered like thirty-some-odd pizzas and enough Chinese food for fifty people." Rafe chuckled.

The thought made Penny smile. "That's something Nicky and Vinnie would do."

Rafe chuckled and nodded. "That's what Logan and I were laughing about. We thought the same thing too." His expression turned solemn. "She's beating herself up over the bioweapon, and zio is letting her. If anything, he pats her on the back, reminds her what an asset she is to the government, then turns around and criticizes every move she makes."

"Savannah was on Serpentine's compound," Penny reminded.

"She went after Mac and fifteen or sixteen other agents," Rafe informed. "We knew Logan was there and injured, but not once did he mention Savannah was there."

Penny sighed and wished she knew what to say. "Zio Lenny thought he was protecting Savannah."

"Maybe," Rafe stated. However, his expression revealed he wasn't convinced. "I think Zio is protecting his self-interest, and Savvy is an afterthought. He's hiding something."

"Like what?" Penny asked and thought of Savannah.

Her brother shook her head. "I don't know, but if Savannah is put in any more danger because of him or caught in the crossfires. I swear to you, Penny, they will never find his body."

Penny absorbed her brother's words. "It's nice to see being in California hasn't changed you."

"Oh, it already has," Rafe assured her with a malicious smile. "It's made me angrier."

Dammit. Just what I need. God help us.

CHAPTER 14

JAVIER WAS glad Penny came down to join the group. She reminded him of a little girl in a lot of ways. There wasn't any doubt that she was close to her brother and Logan. Lennox had made himself scarce. Locked away in his office.

One thing was for sure. The more time Javier spent with Penny, the more attracted he was to her. Maybe he should park on a chair in the hallway. He glanced in the direction of the lab. Savannah had disappeared earlier and hadn't surfaced.

"Is Savannah still in the lab?" Penny asked as if reading his mind.

"Yeah, the warehouse left her with a lot of evidence," Javier admitted.

"Savannah is processing the evidence?" Penny asked again in surprise and another emotion Javier couldn't identify.

"On sensitive cases, yes, especially those connected to the bioweapon," Lewis told her. "Nobody knows that beast like Savvy."

The electronic doors echoed, and Savannah stepped out of the room and glanced around.

A peculiar expression worked across Mac's face. "What wrong, Sugar?"

"I'm just tired," she confessed. "I'm going to get some wine, some air, then go to bed," she told them with a smile, only Javier wasn't buying it for a minute.

"No," Penny sighed. Her gaze was fixed on Savannah. "Something is wrong. Tell us."

Savannah shook her head. "I'm making mistakes, I'm confused, and I need sleep."

Javier darted a glance to Mac. His buddy wasn't buying it, nor was Cowboy or Rafe, who exchanged a look.

Not good. Oh, Savvy, Savvy, what are you not saying?

She removed a bottle from the wine fridge and a goblet from the cupboard. Not a single word left her mouth. However, her mind was deep in thought. Savannah might have been standing a few feet from the table where the group sat in the kitchen, but she was a million miles away.

"Savannah!" Lennox barked from down the hall. His heavy steps thudded against the flooring as he drew near the kitchen, while anger worked Rafe's face.

One day Lennox will snap at Savvy, and her cousin will remove his head.

She poured a small amount of wine into the glass, gulped it back, then placed the goblet down, lifted the bottle, and poured some more into her drink.

"Savannah!" Lennox yelled with a raw temper.

The pretty scientific doctor placed the cork in the bottle and continued to be lost in thought. She lifted her glass and turned around when Lennox entered the kitchen.

"I was calling you," Lennox snapped, glaring at his daughter.

"Yes, you were," Savannah responded calmly. Considering the scientist had a fire when pushed, the tone was too calm.

Like the center of a tornado.

Lennox stepped deeper into the kitchen. "Call the CDC, tell them they're overreacting."

What the hell?

Everyone at the table exchanged looks. Javier had a strange sensation run down his spine.

"No can do," Savannah replied.

She lifted her glass, met her father's gaze over the rim, and smiled. "The way you were yelling like a mad man, you could have raised the dead. We're all alive, though those in the house might be deaf."

Penny's face turned ghost white. "Oh hell," she breathed in a barely audible tone.

Javier would never have heard her if he hadn't been seated next to her. However, on the other side of Penny, Rafe didn't move his head, but instead just his eyes and cast her a sideways glance.

Javier's heart stopped.

Yeah, that's what I thought. They both know something.

The question was, what? And was it the same thing?

Penny buried her head in her hands. "I'm suddenly exhausted."

Considering everything, he was amazed she was still awake. "I'll take you up," Javier assured.

"I've got her," Rafe told him. "I'll be turning in as well. Good night everyone, Zio Lenny," he nodded at Lennox, then Rafe scooped Penny into his arms and exited the kitchen.

Lennox turned to Savannah. "If you're so tired, I suggest you get some sleep." He then turned to the group of agents. "Goodnight, I'll see your ugly mugs in the morning. I'll talk to the group of you then." Lennox then turned and walked down the hallway.

Everyone at the table relaxed except Savannah, who stared at the spot her father had stood. Despite again the close proximity, she again was a million miles away.

Mac was out of his chair and gently held her by her upper arms. "Savannah, now that we're alone, what's wrong?"

"Did you fall for me because Cowboy or my dad said to?"

Oh, not good. Where would she—

"Never," Logan voiced and stepped over to her. "Everyone in this room is asking why you would think that. Ever."

Pain etched in Mac's face. He looked like he'd been sucker punched. Javier couldn't blame him, and his mind immediately went to Penny.

Lennox asked me to do her detail.

Savannah turned to Logan. "Because he's perfect for me."

Cowboy eased her way from Mac and cupped her face. "And you are perfect for him."

Savannah nodded. "I just needed to know."

"I think I fell in love with you the minute you told Darnell and Carter off," Mac grinned and darted a glance to the men at the table, who looked concerned, then returned his attention to Savannah. "I love your dad, but you're my destiny."

Savannah smiled and put her head against Mac's shoulder. "I'm sorry to doubt. I'm just confused."

He wrapped his arms around her protectively. "It's been a long couple of days. Never doubt how much I love you." As if on cue, her breathing fell into a slow steady rhythm. She'd fallen asleep against his friend.

Javier smiled at Mac. "She trusts you."

"And I'll never betray her," Mac stated and turned to Cowboy. "Logan, what don't we know?"

"I'm not sure, but my guess, both girls know, and they are protecting the other or afraid," Cowboy answered with a shake of his head. "Either way, I don't think it's good."

"If I don't miss my guess, it's worse than any of us know," Rafe stated from behind Mac.

Well, that was helpful, said no one. Ever. I thought he was going to bed.

Unfortunately, Javier agreed with Penny's brother.

CHAPTER 15

Penny had removed herself from the bed Rafe had placed her. She wanted to tell her brother everything. However, he couldn't know. None of the family could.

There was movement in the room next door.

"Tu es mon souffle, ma vie et mon amour," Mac voiced.

You are my breath, life, and love.

The words were sincere, it wasn't what was said but the fact it was spoken to her cousin in French. The weight of the world rested on Penny's shoulders. If things had gone different so long ago, Mac would have spoken to her Italian. Heaven knew he was fluent in several languages.

I never would've taken him for such a romantic.

The door of the room next to hers opened and closed again, and she stepped over to the door which connected Penny's room to Savannah's. She quietly opened the door with practiced ease and watched her cousin sleep soundly. Out of everything that had been done, it became more apparent the one they were trying to protect was the one they hurt the most.

I'm sorry, Savvy.

Tonight, something haunted her cousin. Every word and movement after she exited the lab was deliberate. Penny knew that beyond all doubt. Penny as an agent, took that tone and action often, usually before she eliminated a target.

"I know that look, *Mi Reina*," Javier told her quietly. Again calling her his queen.

Penny shook her head. "I don't know how," she whispered.

"That is the face of regret," Javier assured, glancing in the room. "I have younger cousins, remember."

Nodding, Penny shut the door between the rooms and faced Javier. "I fear for her and want to protect her. I sometimes wonder if I should have done more."

Javier's expression held genuine concern. "What's going on?"

"I'm not sure. I know something is distressing Savannah, and I think it's her father." Penny confided quietly. "I don't think she trusts him."

"I don't think she does either," he confessed.

Javier sighed, wrapped an arm around her, and pulled her close to his solid body. "As I said, families are difficult," he whispered, holding her close. "Know above all, I'll keep you safe. Penny, I promise you, whatever you're fighting with inside, you can tell me."

Her heart fluttered.

"I believe you," she whispered and looked up into his handsome face. "What is it about you?" she asked

Javier grinned. "I've wondered the same thing about you." He lowered his head toward her, and Penny closed her eyes.

Hot breath teased her lips as his mouth crushed against hers. Her hands went to his shoulders, and she steadied her body while his hands caressed down her back. The kiss intensified, and she parted her lips to grant his tongue access. Javier's tongue gently explored her mouth and collided with hers as his hands cupped her ass and squeezed.

He lifted his mouth from hers. "This is a terrible idea," he rasped in a husky whisper.

"I know, but it feels right," she breathed.

Javier's firm mouth turned into a grin. "That it does, *Mi Reina*." hesitation worked over his features. "I don't want to hurt you."

Penny met his gaze. "I know you won't. I already know you're like me. You never commit because you'll eventually have to walk away."

"It goes with the job," he confessed. "I almost asked Lewis to take your detail."

Insecurity and doubt worked over Penny. "Why?"

"Because you're the one person I won't be able to walk away from," he told her in all seriousness. "I didn't ask Lewis to swap; instead, I talked to Mac."

Curiosity got the better of her. "What did Mac say?"

"Not giving in to my attraction could be a bigger distraction than not giving in," he answered honestly. "He'd die for Savvy."

"His death would be equal to her own," Penny stated. "I never would have believed aloof Mac would fall so hard for my cousin."

"I can," Javier grinned. "Because I'm falling for you. I mean it, Penny. I won't be able to walk away from you, even when I know you're safe."

"I don't want you to," she whispered. "I haven't felt safe in a long time, years even. The last six months have been hell. However, I wasn't afraid even after we were attacked at the cabin. You were there."

Javier's hold tightened on Penny. "Please, *Mi Reina*, then help me now."

"As much as I want to go for the zipper of your jeans and help you, I don't think that's what you meant," she stated and regretted the words.

"Oh, I appreciate that offer, and after you've

healed a bit more, I will be taking you up on that offer," he answered. "I want to discuss what you remember, from the warehouse to throwing a glass of water at my head."

Penny lightly giggled. "I completely missed you, but I'm sorry for that."

"I think that was the moment I realized you were hurt. You were scared but weren't going out with a fight," Javier told her, and the most fantastic expression crossed his face. "I had so much admiration for you."

"You stole my breath," she admitted. "You're doing it again, right now."

"I should apologize. However, it wouldn't be sincere," Javier nodded. "Can we please talk? You won't say much as long as your brother and cousin are around. Why?" he asked gently.

"I don't want you to think I'm crazy," she confessed, thinking of her hallucinations.

"You're one of the bravest women I have ever met. I know your family has its issues. What are you so afraid of?" Javier still had his arms around her waist, and she placed her head on his shoulder.

"I have moved ever since Serpentine's compound," she replied. "I was on the compound, I followed one of the big-time drug lords from Slovakia, and he stole the scientist helping Serpentine come up with a cure."

Javier released her from his embrace, then

captured his hand in hers and gently had her step away from the dividing door where her cousin slept. Her heart tightened at the thought of her cousin.

"For the last few months, I've been dodging bullets and following a biological weapon. I was almost captured," Penny's voice cracked. "I've been in bad situations but usually not people trying to kidnap me—except for the torture you and until you break scenarios. Which never worked out well for my captors."

"Of course," Javier answered. However, his grief and concern etched into the features of his handsome face.

"This whole thing felt wrong. I had a contact in Prague who told me that the Slovakian drug lord had moved the scientist to American soil and had better come up with results or be executed."

Penny started to shake. "Everything unraveled as I followed the trail," tears burned her eyes, and her voice had turned to water. "I thought the scientist was dead when I reached the warehouse in Bozeman," she lost all control, and a loud sob broke from her throat. The images, the trauma, and the fear all rose to the surface and exploded in an eruption of tears.

Javier's strong arms reached out at the same time. Both doors flung open, and Javier spun Penny behind him and pulled his gun. Logan entered from the hall, and Mac came from the adjoining room with guns drawn. She peeked around Javier's frame as all three men lowered their weapons.

"Sorry," Logan apologized. "You sounded like you were in trouble."

Mac shook his head and sadness blended with confusion.

Javier pulled Penny into his arms as she continued to cry. "She'll be okay," he breathed.

Only Penny wasn't sure. She did know Javier's reflexes were better than most.

"What the hell, Penny?' Logan asked with worry as Rafe walked into the room.

Her brother glanced at her. "I saw the door open. Are you okay?"

She knew she had to get this out, or it would consume her. "Javier was having me open up and tell him what was wrong. I was on American soil because I feared they had Savannah."

"Wow," Javier breathed. "When you asked for your brother, you were hoping to get a message to him."

She nodded. "I was being shadowed, but I don't know by who."

I can't believe I just lied. Sort of.

"While at the warehouse, I discovered it wasn't Savvy. It was the scientist who had tried to come up with a cure for Serpentine's brother. I saw the men in Hazmat suits remove the other scientist, and I entered through the back door. There was a gunfight. One of the arms dealers spotted me and shot at me. He missed, but the bullet ricocheted and hit me. Before I could shoot, he was dead on the floor, and I was bleeding."

Javier released his hold on Penny, and she realized he was easing her down on the sofa in the room's sitting area. "Keep going. You're doing great."

His gentle reassurance had Penny continue. "I tried to get a head start, but the car pulled into the back. The man that put me in the car spoke to a man with a slight accent. Mediterranean, French Riviera. Both spoke English, but one often spoke Italian and the other Old Russian. Only I was delirious because he reminded me so much of Quinn."

"You muttered his name," Javier whispered. "When you slept, kept telling him to go home."

"I know I don't sound lucid," Penny sighed and thought over the particulars of everything she'd experienced.

"Except you know you are and now wondering if he was, how could he walk away from Mel and his friends?" Savannah breathed. "Or one better, was I rescued by ghosts?"

Everyone in the room focused on Penny's cousin, who stood on the threshold. Penny nodded her head. "Did you get a hit on one of the prints?" she asked, remembering her dreams.

"Quinan Romansky, indeed is alive, despite being declared dead." Savannah held out the folder in her hand. "So, the question I have running through my head. How do I tell one of my best friends that her life's love is alive?"

"She moved on pretty fast after Quinn," Mac spoke up as Cowboy took the folder from Savvy.

If Quinn was alive, could....

"I have nothing on some of the others at the scene. I mean that literally," Savannah spoke with conviction. "Some of these players don't exist at first look. So, it's going to take me longer."

"Penny, I don't know why he can't come home, but I think there is a reason. You said you thought it was me. I don't know who the scientist you saw being moved. But I do know this tattoo isn't Russian. She lifted the picture from the top of the now open classified folder in Logan's hand.

Javier stood and took the picture from Savvy. "No, it's Czechoslovakian. Where did you get this Savvy?"

"You were followed, I think," Savannah spoke. "I got thinking about the body temperature of the dead guy at the cabin. He reacted like he'd been dead for hours, full rigor mortis. I think that somehow he's connected to the second scientist."

"Oh my god, you think it's another biological

weapon?" Penny nodded and stepped toward her cousin.

"And now you're starting to think your dad is involved?" Javier finished.

"He knows something because one of the unidentified prints belongs to a Russian drug dealer. A drug bust like twenty- three years ago, and my father signed on the report. He was either FBI or DEA back then. When I know more, I'll let you know."

Holy hell.

"Anyway, I hear spring rolls calling my name from the kitchen," Savannah sighed. "For the record, Mel never moved on from Quinn, despite what it may have looked like."

"Why do I sense there is a story there?" Rafe asked. Surprisingly he had remained quiet up until now.

Savannah turned and blinked at Rafe. "Because you're smart." She then exited the same way she had entered the room from.

Her face tells me much more to that story than she's letting on. The family's going to hate it, I already know. God, she is more like me than I realized.

"How did I get to the cabin in Montana?" Penny asked, and she focused her mind.

"Chuck, a former Navy SEAL, picked you up and brought you to my cabin," Javier replied. "I don't know how. No doubt Lennox was involved.

When I arrived, you were in the guest room, and Chuck, who had been parked on my sofa with a gun out, then returned to his family."

He knew I was in danger.

Javier's words left Penny with little comfort. In fact, now she wondered about the other man who had been in the car. "It's personal. I feel it," she breathed. Suddenly she wasn't worried just about Savannah but her whole family. "A drug bust from so long ago doesn't make sense."

Or it means Zio was really with Quinn.

Penny wasn't sure but seriously wondered.

How?

CHAPTER 16

JAVIER HAD to admit sleeping next to Penny had been fantastic. He woke and discovered her not in bed. Giggles echoed from the room next door, and he hopped off the bed and was glad he wore a tank top and pajama bottoms to bed the night before because Penny had left the adjoining door open.

"Oh, I love this sweater," Penny exclaimed.

His heart relaxed a bit, hearing the happiness in her voice.

"I love you being here," Savannah confided. "You'd look pretty in it with your hair."

"I'm sure Zio Lenny or Rafe have notified my mom," Penny sighed. "I like being here. I may stay on after the lockdown for a couple extra days."

Javier couldn't help but smile and liked the idea of her being around. He looked in the room and spotted the two girls by the closet door.

"I think you should stay," Savannah smiled like a pretty devil. "Especially since you have a bodyguard here, and he's gorgeous."

"You're meddling, Savvy," Javier called as he leaned against the door frame.

"I'm not," Savannah replied, glancing his way. "I was merely mentioning one of your finer qualities."

Javier chuckled and nodded, then met Penny's gaze. Her color was better, and she looked happy. "I'm going to get ready. I'll meet you downstairs."

"I'll see you then," Penny told him.

Javier peeled himself away from the door and hit the shower. When he came down the stairs, he noticed the guys sitting around the table—including Rafe. "Good morning," he greeted and walked over to the coffee pot.

"I think you should tell her," Mac sighed, glancing at Rafe. "She has a right to know, at least start with what she knows."

"Who, what, when, and where's the boss?" Javier asked.

"Zio Lenny is with his new recruits. I would've fired the pants wetter. I don't think a federal agent should demonstrate such fear," Rafe answered. "As for who, what, when, well, that depends on your intentions with my sister."

"I'm her bodyguard," Javier assured the man as he poured a coffee and then turned to the group of men.

"Yes, but she trusts you," Rafe stated and glanced over the rim of his mug. "In my family, that is worth more than gold."

Nodding, Javier could understand that.

The automatic doors opening from down the hall echoed through the kitchen. Both Penny and Savannah walked into the room. In Savannah's hand was a piece of paper which she passed to Penny, who walked over to the table. An unreadable expression was on Penny's face, and she met Rafe's gaze and shook her head no.

Savannah walked over to the refrigerator, placed her hand on the handle, and paused.

"What's wrong?" Javier asked the quiet scientist.

She turned around and glanced at the table. Her glance went to the kitchen entrance, then looked at Lewis. "The last time this room became quiet when I walked in the room, Cowboy had just arrived, and Lewis stormed past him pissed."

Rafe glanced to Mac, who shook his head. "I wasn't here," he told Penny's brother.

"No, you were on the compound," she stated with a slight quiver in her voice. "So let's cut through the chase since you're all here."

Javier had to admit that his question or questions had still gone unanswered.

Lewis picked up the paper, looked at it, and then placed it down. He inhaled a breath and met

Savannah's gaze. Every nerve in Javier's body went on alert. "This links Dr. Bobik, a Czech scientist, to creating an extra human?"

Penny shook her head. "Neobyčejný člověk is Czech and actually translates to extraordinary human. Yeah, there is another bio-weapon out there. It's what Quinn and Matteo were chasing in Russia. All I could find in my research is there were several attempts; seventy-two men died throughout the testing. Three survived."

"Well, I have a feeling Creepy One and Creepy Two in the morgue are part of the survivors' group," Javier said sarcastically.

"Wonderful, two down the third to go, and we have no idea where he might be," Cowboy voiced.

Mac sighed. "We were talking about what you and Penny have pieced together," Mac stated and exchanged glances with Rafe and then Cowboy. He then turned back to Savannah. "We think Penny's right, and it's personal."

"I feel it," Penny assured.

Peirce's instincts are at play. I have no doubt she's right.

Hesitation worked over Mac's face. "What do you know about your mother?"

Surprise revealed itself on Savannah's face, and she frowned. "She died when I was three. I don't remember her. She was French, so dad wanted me to go to Joan of Arc French Immersion and learn the language my mother spoke. I know dad said they never got the driver who hit her."

"Driver?" Mac asked.

Savannah nodded, and a sad expression crossed her face. "My mom died in a car accident, ran off the road, died on impact. It was a hit and run," she explained.

Javier was reading Mac, he knew something, but Javier had no clue what that might be. Interesting, Cowboy nor Moretti spoke. One thing Javier was good at was reading a room. He turned to Savannah. "Did you ever pull up the case file?"

"I tried too a few years back," Savannah admitted and glanced at Javier. "Only I couldn't pull it up. I asked dad about it, but he said he was with the FBI, and they sometimes bury or delete files to keep their agent's identity a secret."

Javier darted a look to the others. Yeah, it could be, but something told Javier there was another reason.

Like it never existed.

Inhaling deep, Savannah studied the group at the table. "Do you think it's connected?"

Silence.

"No, Sugar, probably not," Mac assured. "We are just going everything and not leaving a stone unturned. Safety precaution."

"Sorry, I'm no more help," she replied and returned to the refrigerator. She grabbed a bottle of juice. "If you need me, I'm processing evidence." Her phone rang from her pocket. She glanced at the number, and dread worked across her face. "Oh dear," she whispered in defeat. She forced a smile and answered the phone. "Hey Mel, what's up?" she greeted in an everything-is-fine tone.

How does she do that?

Savannah walked out of the room. "How is my gorgeous goddaughter?" she asked into the phone as she stepped back toward the lab.

Javier blew out a breath. No one spoke until the sound of the lab's mechanical opening, and closing was complete, and the lock latched.

Penny buried her head and hands, and Javier placed the mug down he'd held in his hand. He crossed over to where she sat when her shoulders lifted and then fell in a soft sob.

Hell. This is not good.

Crouching down next to Penny, he brushed her auburn hair back off her face. "What's going on, *Mi Reina*?" he asked softly. He still didn't understand what was going on around him.

Penny met his gaze, and tears ran down her pretty face. "He lied to her," she breathed, then threw her arms around Javier's neck.

Javier wrapped his arms around her and held

her for a minute. "We'll figure this out, I promise you. We'll keep you and Savvy safe." He eased her back a bit. "The hall bathroom outside of the lab, Savannah uses. Go freshen up so she doesn't see you upset, okay? In the meantime, I'll have the guys bring me up to speed."

She kissed his cheek, got up from the table, and hurried toward the restroom. Javier came to a standing position.

"Calling my sister a *queen* is touching. Never forget why you've given her that name," Rafe stated calmly—too calmly. No mistake which side of the family Savannah got that from. "Please, always cherish her."

Javier met the other man's gaze. "Not a problem. I'm gathering Lennox lied to Savannah about her mother. My question is, why?"

"We don't know. It can go with the restraining order and all the other fucking crap that man does," Rafe exclaimed in frustration. He pushed back the chair and stood. Slowly he walked to the patio doors and stared out them.

Javier noted the gun at the back waist of Rafe's jeans. Something about the way Dr. Moretti stood didn't seem to fit. He was a capo for the mob, but he didn't come off that way right now. Rafe was pissed off older cousin and brother.

Crossing the floor to where Rafe stood, Javier

understood that protective streak better than anyone. "What restraining order?"

Rafe met his gaze in the reflection of the glass patio doors. "After my Aunt Gia was killed, Zio Lenny packed up a three-year-old Savannah and moved her from New York to Beverly Hills. He wanted nothing to do with his friends and family. The only one he stayed in contact with was Zio Carlo."

Cowboy's dad.

The restraining order listed almost everyone, except my mother, sister, and me," Rafe informed. "My own father wasn't allowed to see Savannah."

Javier turned and glanced to Cowboy, who nodded it was true. Beside him, Mac looked like he'd been punched and stood from his chair. His cowboy boots scuffed the floor as he paced. There was no secret. Mac had looked at Lennox like a father.

If he didn't miss his guess, Javier suspected Mac was as livid as Rafe. Savannah was the Supervisory Agent's life. "Talk to us, Mac," Javier called out and looked at his friend.

"We can't figure things out if we don't know the truth or who could be doing this, and right now, I don't think I can trust Lennox." The anger in his tone wasn't hard to miss.

"I think we can all agree on this," Lewis stated.

"The question is—" The sound of Savannah coming out of her lab echoed down the hall.

"Mel, there is nothing here," she assured. "I have no idea what you're talking about. Hang on." She looked at the group and then the heavy metal door on the other side of the kitchen. "Is there anyone in the Inner Agency Communication Network?"

"No," Lewis answered with a shake of his head. "Why?'

"Mel says there is a communication signal they can't identify being picked up on a foreign satellite," Savannah informed, then repositioned the phone. "Can they figure out where it's coming from on the compound?"

Penny stepped back into the room with freshly applied makeup. Immediately she crossed over to where Javier stood with her brother.

"Where is my father?" Savannah asked the room.

"Nevada with the new recruits," Darnell answered.

Savannah shook her head. "Nevada," she spoke into the phone. "With his new recruits, including a pants wetter," Savannah complained. "Apparently, the agent-want-to-be has a real problem following orders."

There was a pause.

"I did nothing but read the little bitch the riot act," Savannah explained. "I did nothing, really."

There was another pause. “Okay, so maybe I throat pinned him to a wall while giving the riot act. I promise you, Mel, I’m working on my people skills.”

The agents around the room snickered.

Rafe burst out laughing and ran his hands over his face, then glanced at Savannah over his fingers. He stepped over to Mac. “I want you to know I’m sorry I called you a chooch. You should be given a medal.”

“God, I love her,” Mac admitted quietly.

A thoughtful expression crossed his face. “I know. You have no reason to believe me, but my family wants her in their lives. They never wanted to let her go,” he whispered.

“I swear, Mac, he isn’t lying,” Cowboy assured in a husky voice.

Savannah walked down the hallway toward her father’s office and then stopped in the hallway. “There is nothing on.”

Suddenly the alarms on the compound went off.

“Carter! Darnell! We have a problem at the front gate,” an agent called over the speakers.

“What kind of problem?” Darnell asked with an aggressive edge to his tone.

“Sir, a crazy man is, what the hell…?” the sound of bullets firing echoed.

“Proceed with lockdown protocol,” Lewis barked.

"Mel, get SWAT here now!" Savannah spun around and glanced at the group; horror washed over her face. "What do you mean it's coming from the morgue?'"

Javier closed his eyes. What the hell was going on?

CHAPTER 17

PENNY RUSHED to Savannah as the monitors in the hallway flickered on. "Initiating security protocol," the automated voice from when she first arrived kicked on. "Front gate has experienced seventy-five percent damage, bringing upfront gate camera."

"What kind of signal?" Penny asked as the group of men gathered around the monitors.

"Satellite signal," her cousin whispered, with a hint of fear in her tone. "I think there is something in one of the bodies downstairs," she confessed. "If that is even possible." Her gaze turned to the monitor near the elevator. The gate was bent as if something had hit hard, yet no vehicles were present. A large man walked in front of the camera, then turned and stared at the camera. Blood ran down his face like crimson tears. His nose and ears bled as he lifted the gun and shot the camera.

“That is terrifying,” Carter whispered. “He’s infected with Malebola.”

Rafe turned to Penny with a look of question in his gaze. She nodded her head. Yes, this is the weapon she’d been involved with from day one. The extraordinary humans. Yes, the Malebola was their sweet cousin’s biggest mistake. Yes, she was scared but had faith things would be fine.

“Security seal initiated,” the automated voice announced s dark shades dropped over the patio doors off the kitchen and the windows.

Next to Penny, Savannah’s back stiffened. “I understand now what you mean about the zombie. He shouldn’t be doing that.”

“Then why the hell is he?” Agent Jared Carter asked. “This is impossible.”

Rafe turned to Javier. “You said the one behind the cabin had ripped a tree out?”

“Uh, yes, with his bare hands, right before he tried throwing it at me,” Javier answered.

Cowboy nodded, looked from Javier to the screen, and then lifted his brows. “This guy mangled the iron gate with his bare hands?”

“That would be a safe bet,” Penny breathed. “Good news, boys, I think we found the third, extraordinary human.”

Cowboy exchanged a glance with Mac. “I see the family resemblance. How about you?”

“Oh, yeah,” Mac breathed. “Sarcastic to the hilt.”

"I love sarcasm," Javier added.

"We know," Carter, Darnell, Cowboy, and Mac replied.

Under normal conditions, Penny would have laughed. Today wasn't typical. Her last few days hadn't been. However, she believed in what her nonna had always said. "Tutto per una ragione," she breathed.

Savannah turned and smiled, then nodded. "Everything for a reason." She stepped away from Penny and looked at Mac. "What do you suggest?"

"Rafe and I will deal with the signal going off in the morgue," Mac began.

Javier nodded. "Lewis, get on the Inner Agency Communication Network and coordinate with Melanie." He turned to his cousin Jared. "You and Darnell get out there and see who on grounds guard is still alive and work with Lewis on getting medical personnel where needed."

Penny turned to Javier. "What are you going to do?"

He grinned and smiled. "Make sure Humanzilla doesn't kill you or Savvy."

"I like that idea," Savannah agreed as a loud thud came to the front door. "Oh, dear."

Oh, dear, that is right. What is my luck with bioweapon-infected zombies?

Penny made a silent deal that if she lived through this, she would take time off to heal and spend time with her younger cousin. “Tell me there is some decent firepower around here?”

Savannah nodded and hurried past Javier into the kitchen. “Time to raid the pantry.”

Not what I was thinking,

“Really, Savvy? You think now’s the time to have a snack,” Penny complained, following close on her cousin’s heels.

Savannah walked over to the pantry, opened the door then flipped up the small panel next to it. A light came on, and she scanned her eye.

“Why do you have all the cool toys?” Penny asked as the food on the shelves parted and revealed a small artillery room. Penny glanced at her cousin as Savannah grabbed a handgun and a giant taser. “I so am hanging out here more.”

Javier chuckled and grabbed what looked like a small rocket launcher. “I think that’s a good idea. This house has all the good stuff.”

The banging continued, and metal bending echoed through the house.

“SWAT is two minutes out,” Lewis’s voice informed over the speaker system as he appeared on the screens near the elevator and in the hallway.

Javier wheeled around and glared at the screen. “This will be over in thirty seconds. A little help would be great.”

Lewis surfaced out of the Inner Agency Communication Network and grabbed a large rifle. The hinges on the front entrance started pulling away from the wood. The sound splintered through the air.

"We'll give you cover," Lewis called and grabbed Savvy by the wrist, then kicked in one of the doors of Lenny's office. Savvy took cover behind the one side of the double doors still shut, cocked her gun, and turned the taser on, while Lewis dropped to a knee on the other side and then positioned the rifle.

Penny held her breath as she stepped into the kitchen and leaned against the wall. She glanced to Javier, who had the small rocket ready. A loud alarm filled the speaker system. "Fire detected in the medical lab," the automated voice announced.

What the hell are Mac and my brother doing down there?

"Fire contained and emergency response activated, estimated time seven minutes," the automated voice reported as the front door fell straight back to the floor.

So much for the good news.

The large body stepped through, walking over the door on the threshold.

"Electricity," Rafe barked over the speaker system.

The humanzilla stared at Javier. Suddenly two electric cords shot out from Zio Lenny's office without a doubt attached to the taser Savannah had swiped. The zombie shook and trembled.

"I can't believe he's still standing.," Penny breathed in horror.

"Tell me about it," Javier agreed.

The gun in the hand of the creature, bleeding but still not dead, went off. Penny aimed for the head and pulled the trigger. Down the hall, the rifle fired two shots.

As the monster started to fall forward, Javier lowered the lever, and a small rocket launched down the hallway. It connected with the beast and knocked him back through the door and onto the driveway. Siren's blared closer, and Penny leaned against the wall.

"Confirmed kill," Darnell's voice yelled as Rafe and Mac hurried through the stairwell door and into the kitchen.

Javier stepped over to Penny. "Are you okay?" he asked and cupped her face as, with guns drawn, Mac and Rafe proceeded with caution down the hall toward Zio Lenny's office.

"I will be," Penny replied and buried her head into Javier's shoulder, his arms wrapped around her waist.

"Your safe," Javier whispered gently.

Penny closed her eyes and didn't want to move.

"My dad is going to have my ass for this one," Savvy exclaimed.

Penny lifted her head and glanced to where her cousin was with Rafe and Mac. Rafe wrapped an arm around Savannah. "Don't worry about it. I know a guy."

Mac came to a stop and exchanged a look with Javier. "Of course you do," Mac chuckled.

"I do. A couple calls, and there will be a new door in record time," Rafe assured, then shrugged. "I need a bit longer to get a new MRI machine."

"What did you two do to the MRI machine?" Savannah asked in a panic.

Mac and Rafe exchanged a guilty look, then glanced at Savannah. "We figured the easiest and fastest way to kill the signal if it was in the extraordinary humans was with magnetic resonance imagery," Rafe explained, "Those machines don't like metal."

Javier laughed and grinned at Penny. "Good news Mi Reina, we now know what caused the fire downstairs."

Though their idea had worked, she couldn't imagine how much the damages would run. On the bright side, Penny and the others were too old to get grounded.

At least, she hoped.

CHAPTER 18

Penny stepped into the room next to Savannah's. Her cousin had been asleep for a couple of hours now. The dust had settled, and federal agents were on every inch of the grounds. True to her brother's word, within the hour of Rafe calling home. Repair crews started work on fixing the house.

At least there was a new door.

If Penny had learned anything over the last few days, Savannah needed family more than ever. Javier shut the room door and came up next to where Penny stood.

"Maybe you should stay on after the CDC eases the quarantine," Javier breathed. His hand reached up and cupped her cheek. "I'll be with you, even when we are free to leave. I can't leave you until you and your family are safe, and I couldn't leave you if I tried."

Javier's words melted Penny. She turned and met his dark gaze. "She needs me," Penny whispered.

"As do I, *Mi Reina*," he answered, and his thumb gently brushed her skin.

She stared at the man in front of her and covered his mouth with hers. Javier's arms went around her while his lips and tongue deepened the kiss. She grasped his strong shoulders in her hands as he roamed over her body.

With care, his touch explored her body. Penny reached for his t-shirt and removed it from the waist of Javier's jeans before tugging it all the way up and over his head. Once his shirt was gone, he captured the ends of her sweater and tossed it to the side.

His strong hands grasped her hips, then he walked her backward until the edge of the bed caught her behind the knee, and Penny fell back. Javier slowly worked her out of her jeans and her undergarments. He smiled as he stood, removed the rest of his clothes, stretched his body over Penny's, and dipped a hand between her legs.

Her pussy twitched, and desire dampened his touch. Gasping, she tilted her head back as he repositioned himself between her legs. Her knees separated, and the tip of his cock teased her sensitive entrance. The head of Javier's thick dick separated her wet walls as he buried himself inside.

Penny paused a moment, and he leaned by her ear. "Am I hurting you?" he asked in a seductive whisper.

"No," she breathed and wiggled her hips beneath him. Slowly Javier started working his length in and out of her, taking cautionary thrusts so as not to jolt her torso too bad. Again she rocked her hips and wanted more of him.

Javier groaned and slowly picked up speed. Without causing too much strain to her recovering wound, Penny met his thrusts as the pressure slowly built in her pelvis. His hot mouth crushed against her lips, and his tongue thrust into her mouth.

Every inch of Penny's body blazed in desire as Javier worked her mouth and wet core with deliberation. His thrusts became deeper and faster. The sensations of Javier ignited through her body, and she broke the kiss as her shoulders lifted off the bed. Her tongue collided with his as her body trembled in a release.

A feral groan escaped Javier against her mouth as he thrust one last time. His body stiffened, and she laced her arms around his neck while his dick emptied inside her pulsing wet walls.

Javier struggled for breath and buried his face in her hair. "I love you," he rasped in a husky whisper.

"I love you too," she assured and closed her eyes, trying to shut out the horrors of her day.

His large frame slid off her and rested on the other side of the bed. Javier pulled her close to his side as Penny's eyelids became heavier. She curled into her bodyguard's side, placed a hand on his chest, and savored the moment.

Despite the hell, Penny had experienced. She now knew she'd never be alone with Javier by her side.

CHAPTER 19

Javier glanced to the other side of the bed. Penny slept soundly. He leaned over and brushed her hair off her cheek. She sighed with contentment, and Javier placed a kiss on her cheek. A smile curled across her lips, and he wished her peaceful dreams with the hope they included him.

He pulled on his clothes and snuck over to the adjoining door. Quietly he opened it to see Savannah asleep and no sign of Mac. Javier again shut the door and crossed to the entrance, which led to the hallway. He crossed the threshold and glanced at Yuri.

"I've got them," he assured. There was a new edge to his tone. "The others are in the kitchen."

Javier hurried toward the landing.

"Javier," Yuri called. "Help bring Quinn home."

"I promise," he told the other man. His mind

went to Melanie McCormick and her young daughter. "What were you thinking, Quinn? Leaving them in a world without you," he muttered as his steps carried him downstairs, through the hallway, and into the kitchen.

Cowboy, Mac, Lewis, Darnell, and his cousin Jared Carter sat around the table. What surprised him in a small way was that Rafael Moretti sat with them. "So this is how it's going to be?" Javier asked of Penny's brother.

Rafe met his gaze. "I don't see another way, do you?"

"No," Javier replied in complete honesty. "I don't trust Lennox."

Rafe sighed. "So we are all in agreement?"

Every man agreed, and Javier pulled up a chair. "So, what's the plan?"

"Cowboy and Lewis are going to retrace Penny's steps," Rafe began. "I need you to go with Penny and find out what Chuck Johnson knows. He has to know something we don't."

Javier thought of the older Navy SEAL. "He's a good man."

Rafe shook his head. "Of that, I have little doubt. Carter and Darnell are going to cover our favorite scientist, but I want Penny on hand after you two talk to Chuck, which will give us some time to fill in missing pieces and hopefully help Savannah deal with the guilt she carries over the weapon."

Cowboy cleared his throat. "Mac has suggested moving Penny to intelligence, let her recover, and liaison with Melanie."

"I like this," Javier admitted. "I think the cousins need each other. Savannah needs reassurance, and Penny needs to know her young cousin is safe and within reach."

Rafe sighed. "Protect them," he breathed. "I need to brief Padrino. There is too much unknown and too much on the line for an error."

"I concur," Javier told the man. "What about Quinn?"

"We will deal with the situation abroad," Lewis assured. "Back up the others with whatever they need, and Rafe will bring la famiglia in when needed."

A weighted sigh echoed from the hallway entrance. "Well, doesn't circumstance ignite the most interesting bedfellows?"

Javier turned and smiled at Penny, who leaned against the wall. "Indeed, *Mi Reina*."

Right now, he had more trust in the men at the table than the man who'd picked up Javier's training where Chuck left off.

Beyond all reason, Javier knew he was making the best choice. The one that would keep his queen safe.

CHAPTER 20

JAVIER GLANCED around his cabin in Montana. He couldn't believe it was only a couple weeks since he'd arrived at a dying Penny in his guest room and Chuck seated on his sofa. Everything had been restored, cleaned, and repaired. It was perfect.

Except for hand tied quilt on the bed in the room Penny had been in. It now resided on the bed in the room next to Savannah's at Lennox's compound. The cousins had become closer. Rafe had agreed keeping Penny and Savannah together was safer until they could figure out the attack on the family. "You'd never know we had killed bioweapon infected zombies here."

Penny grinned. "What can I say? My zio knows a guy."

He started to laugh. "You do that with such a

Staten Island accent. I appreciate them doing this. It was nice of your family."

"I now Rafe put in a good word for you," she admitted. "I'm glad we're here now. How do you think Savvy is?"

Of course, she's worried. Savannah still doesn't know the truth about her mother.

All in good time.

"She's in good hands, and as we speak, she is safe. Lenny is still at his training sight in Nevada with the new recruits. The guys were going to handle our problem outside of Prague."

A vehicle pulled up, and Penny and Javier reached for their guns. He slipped to the large window and glanced around the blinds. "It's only Chuck," Javier informed as a knock rapped against the screen door.

His body relaxed. "Come on in," Javier called and stepped back near Penny.

The screen door sound echoed, and Chuck walked over the threshold. "I'm glad to see the both of you," he greeted and smiled at Penny. "You look better than the last time I saw you."

"Sir," Javier greeted and crossed the floor to the man he adored. "Please, sit," he invited and waved to a chair.

Penny hung her head as she and Javier sat on the sofa. "We need your help."

"What's going on?" his mentor and, in some ways, his savior asked.

Javier met the gaze of the man who broke him, only to rebuild him into the man he was today. "I need to ask for your discretion."

Chuck studied Javier with a look that penetrated him to his soul. "What's going on?" Chuck didn't even blink, but the concern was in his eyes.

"We think someone is targeting Zio Lenny; his life is in danger," Penny explained.

"He'd call me," Chuck assured.

"I don't think so," Penny sighed, and Javier pulled her close. "Not this time. I don't think he is even privy to the information."

"The real reason we're here is that we need to know what information you have on *The Ghost*," Javier asked.

"Nothing and maybe everything," Javier's mentor revealed. "When agents on and off the books need help, he's there when hope is gone." He smiled like a cat with a canary. "My turn. Why are you asking me these questions and not your uncle?" His gaze rested on Penny.

"Because whoever is gunning for Zio Lenny has other targets in mind, and we need to identify them. We believe my younger cousin Savannah is in bigger danger than we realized." Penny swallowed hard. "I've lost enough in my life. I don't want to lose her," she voiced in cracked emotion. "I can't lose her."

A thoughtful expression and a touch of sadness worked over Chuck's features.

Javier's heart hurt. He knew this conversation was complicated for Penny but also for Chuck. He'd lost more than most and understood all too well. "You're probably wondering why we're asking."

"You could say that," Chuck informed in his patience-is-thinning tone.

"Because the only thing linking this man to Lennox is a drug bust over two decades ago," Penny informed. "No name, no face, fingerprints of a ghost."

"Why would I know?" his mentor asked.

Javier smiled. "I know you're former DEA."

Chuck nodded his head. "As I said, *Ghost* is there when agents need him, then vanishes as quickly as he appeared. He has literally surfaced all over the country and globally. No one knows how he gets his information, but he has remarkable timing and is considered an ally. He isn't the one after your family."

Penny nodded, and Javier held her hand. "Then who?"

The older man shook his head. "That I don't know, but I'll help you find out anyway I can."

Javier squeezed Penny's hand in reassurance and turned to the woman he loved. "We'll figure this out."

Hopefully, sooner rather than later.

ABOUT KANDI SILVERS

♥

Born and raised in Las Vegas, Nevada, I still call Sin City home. I've always been a sucker for romance novels and movies, especially romantic comedies. Writing is more than words; it captures slices of characters' lives and shares them with the reader. I firmly believe that heroes and heroines had a life before page one of any story and their past and life experiences made them who they are.

Coming from the southwest, I have a soft spot for cowboys, but I also love suspense, a bit of intrigue, and kick-ass heroines. Of course, there is always the time to slip in a good paranormal. I try to keep my writing diverse and always on the naughty side. Happy reading!

~Kisses,

Kandi

For more ***Girls With Guns*** check out my website:
www.kandisilversauthor.com

BROTHERHOOD PROTECTORS

ORIGINAL SERIES BY ELLE JAMES

Brotherhood Protectors Series

Montana SEAL (#1)

Bride Protector SEAL (#2)

Montana D-Force (#3)

Cowboy D-Force (#4)

Montana Ranger (#5)

Montana Dog Soldier (#6)

Montana SEAL Daddy (#7)

Montana Ranger's Wedding Vow (#8)

Montana SEAL Undercover Daddy (#9)

Cape Cod SEAL Rescue (#10)

Montana SEAL Friendly Fire (#11)

Montana SEAL's Mail-Order Bride (#12)

SEAL Justice (#13)

Ranger Creed (#14)

Delta Force Rescue (#15)

Dog Days of Christmas (#16)

Montana Rescue (#17)

Montana Ranger Returns (#18)

Hot SEAL Salty Dog (SEALs in Paradise)

Hot SEAL Hawaiian Nights (SEALs in Paradise)

Hot SEAL Bachelor Party (SEALs in Paradise)

ABOUT ELLE JAMES

ELLE JAMES also writing as MYLA JACKSON is a *New York Times* and *USA Today* Bestselling author of books including cowboys, intrigues and paranormal adventures that keep her readers on the edges of their seats. When she's not at her computer, she's traveling, snow skiing, boating, or riding her ATV, dreaming up new stories. Learn more about Elle James at www.ellejames.com

Website | Facebook | Twitter | GoodReads | Newsletter | BookBub | Amazon

Or visit her alter ego Myla Jackson at mylajackson.com
Website | Facebook | Twitter | Newsletter

Follow Me!
www.ellejames.com
ellejamesauthor@gmail.com

www.ingramcontent.com/pod-product-compliance
Lightning Source LLC
LaVergne TN
LVHW050545160826
845677LV00011B/2191

* 9 7 9 8 8 4 6 6 9 4 3 4 7 *